W9-COI-045

LAND OF THE LOST

Frank stared down from the wall at the yard below. It was almost empty, except for a stone sculpture of a small dinosaur at one end, away from the building.

Before Frank could say anything, Joe jumped off the wall, somersaulting as he landed and rolling to his feet. Frank shrugged and jumped too, landing the same way his brother had.

"Now let's see if we can find a way in," Frank said. "Maybe around back—"

"Frank." Joe's arm shot out across his brother's chest, stopping Frank dead in his tracks. He pointed across the yard. "I don't think that's a statue."

The statue was moving toward them.

"It's alive," Frank said, not believing his own words. He watched the creature as it came closer to them. It had to be at least eight feet long and weigh several hundred pounds. "That's no dinosaur . . . it's a Komodo dragon . . . a man-eater!"

Books in THE HARDY BOYS CASEFILES® Series

Available from ARCHWAY Paperbacks

THE HARDY BOYS CASEFILES

No. 78

RING OF EVIL 3

THE PACIFIC CONSPIRACY

FRANKLIN W. DIXON

Eau Claire District Library

AN ARCHWAY PAPERBACK
Published by POCKET BOOKS
New York   London   Toronto   Sydney   Tokyo   Singapore

88756

The sale of this book without its cover is unauthorized. If you purchased this book without a cover, you should be aware that it was reported to the publisher as "unsold and destroyed." Neither the author nor the publisher has received payment for the sale of this "stripped book."

This book is a work of fiction. Names, characters, places and incidents are either products of the author's imagination or are used fictitiously. Any resemblance to actual events or locales or persons, living or dead, is entirely coincidental.

AN ARCHWAY PAPERBACK *Original*

An Archway Paperback published by
POCKET BOOKS, a division of Simon & Schuster Inc.
1230 Avenue of the Americas, New York, NY 10020

Copyright © 1993 by Simon & Schuster Inc.
Produced by Mega-Books of New York, Inc.

All rights reserved, including the right to reproduce this book or portions thereof in any form whatsoever. For information address Pocket Books, 1230 Avenue of the Americas, New York, NY 10020

ISBN: 0-671-79462-0

First Archway Paperback printing August 1993

10 9 8 7 6 5 4 3 2 1

THE HARDY BOYS, AN ARCHWAY PAPERBACK and colophon are registered trademarks of Simon & Schuster Inc.

THE HARDY BOYS CASEFILES is a trademark of Simon & Schuster Inc.

Cover art by Brian Kotzky

Printed in the U.S.A.

IL 6+

Chapter

1

"MAN, IT'S JUST too hot," seventeen-year-old Joe Hardy said, setting down his groceries on the sidewalk. He wiped his face with the bottom of his T-shirt, which was already soaked.

People rushed by him on the crowded sidewalk, streaming in and out of the entrance to the supermarket. None of them, Joe noted crossly, seemed to be sweating, which made him feel even more conspicuous than ever. Of course, being six feet tall with blond hair, he would stand out among these people anyway. Almost everyone around him was shorter and darker. Then again, this was Djakarta, the capital of Indonesia, so what did he expect?

The natives must be used to the heat, he thought, picking up his groceries and cradling

1

them in his arms. How anyone could get used to ninety-degree heat and ninety-percent humidity he didn't know. At eleven in the morning, it already was so hot he'd have bet he could fry an egg on the sidewalk.

Not that people in Indonesia ate eggs. At least, not the people he was with. Grapefruit and tea was all the Assassins seemed to need. Joe was ready to kill for a hamburger about now.

He shook his head to clear it. This was no time to think about food. He and his older brother, Frank, were in the middle of the most dangerous case of their lives. Through a remarkable series of events they had managed to infiltrate the Assassins, the deadliest group of terrorists in the world. The Assassins were a group of fanatics who, Joe knew, wouldn't think twice about killing him or his brother if they found out who they really were. Joe and Frank were actually working for the Network, a top-secret U.S. government organization.

No one would believe that a couple of teenagers such as Joe and Frank were government agents. They weren't, really. The whole thing had started with their doing a little preliminary detective work for their father, the world-famous private investigator Fenton Hardy.

The boys had been flown down to Atlanta, Georgia, to check out a series of luggage thefts plaguing Eddings Air. As they were uncovering the luggage theft ring they ran into the Assassins, who were trying to steal one piece of luggage—a fly fishing rod case containing notes describing a breakthrough discovery by Dr. Nikolai Stavrogin.

Dr. Stavrogin, Frank and Joe had discovered, was one of their country's foremost nuclear physicists. He had come up with a simple new method for creating an uncontrolled fusion reaction, which is what a hydrogen bomb blast is. Joe didn't entirely understand the method, but he knew the equations made it possible for the Assassins, with the right materials, to make a thermonuclear device of massive power. The Assassins had kidnapped Dr. Stavrogin, who later had been rescued by the Hardys and the Network.

Joe and Frank, along with Gina Abend, an employee of Eddings Air, had trailed the Assassins to Alaska. Although they had rescued Dr. Stavrogin from the terrorists, they failed to prevent the death of Gina, Joe noted sadly.

He and Frank had conned the terrorists into accepting them into their group. The Assassins had brought them first to Hawaii and then to Indonesia, where they'd spent the past two weeks sitting around. The most exciting thing they had allowed Joe to do was shop for groceries that day. Hardly terrorist work, Joe thought.

Just then someone slammed into his right arm, and Joe dropped his groceries.

"Maaf!"

He turned to see a young woman shaking her

head at the groceries, which were spilled all over the sidewalk.

"Saya kurang mengerti," Joe replied. It was the only Indonesian he knew. It meant, "I don't understand."

"Ah," the woman said. *"Apa saudara dapat bitiara bahasa Inggeris?"*

Joe shook his head. "I don't get that either."

"I asked if you spoke English," she said, smiling. "I said I was sorry also," she added, kneeling down on the sidewalk. She began picking up his produce and stuffing it back into the bag. "I was in a hurry."

"I didn't see you, either," Joe said. And no wonder. She was barely five feet tall, about his age, with long black hair, a round, pretty face, and caramel-colored skin.

"You're an American," she said.

"That's right," he answered. "Joe Hardy."

"Endang Merdeka." She popped the last grapefruit back into the grocery bag, then stood and smoothed her long, colorful skirt. "What brings you to Indonesia, Joe?"

Joe shrugged. "Touring the sights."

"The grocery stores?" she said, shaking her head. "You ought to spend your time here doing things more unique to our country. Have you eaten *padang* yet? Or seen the *wayang kulit?*"

"No," Joe admitted.

Endang frowned. "What you need is a guide." She reached into her bag and pulled out a yellow handbill. There was a drawing of two strange, distorted figures on it. "There is a *wayang kulit* performance tonight at our national art center, the TIM. You can meet me there at eight."

She turned the handbill over. "It's easy to find," she said, scribbling down directions with a pen. "Tonight. Eight o'clock. You won't forget, will you?"

Joe shrugged helplessly. The truth was, he would have loved to go, even though he didn't know what a *wayang kulit* was, but the Assassins would never let him. He was surprised they had left him alone this long at the store.

Even more surprising was their allowing Frank to remain on the boat alone that morning. Joe didn't believe for a second that Frank had an upset stomach. Frank was up to something, he was sure of it.

"It's very important that you come, Joe," Endang said.

"Hardy! Where are you?" a voice called out before he could answer her.

Joe recognized that voice. It belonged to Boris, one of the Assassins. Boris had pretended to be unable to speak much English when they first met. Joe now knew it was so he could spy on Joe and Frank, because not only could the man speak English, he also was an American.

Joe turned in time to see the giant walking toward him. Not a real giant, of course, but at six feet, four inches tall, the bearded Assassin towered over the Indonesians rushing by him.

He and Frank had met Boris in Alaska. That was his entire name—Boris. It was an alias, just like the names of the other Assassins they'd met there, Bob and Bill. All three were with them in Indonesia, along with two other terrorists, one of whom was named Butch.

Joe was half expecting that he and Frank would be expected to change their names to Buck and Buddy.

Boris was scowling at Joe. He was probably angry because Joe hadn't waited for him inside the store.

Joe was more frightened of the guy coming out of the store behind Boris, though.

"Joseph," was all the newcomer said.

This man didn't look like much of a threat at first glance. A few inches shorter than Joe, in his midforties, whipcord thin, with graying hair and mustache, he was pretty nondescript. Until you focused on his eyes.

The irises were almost completely black. They were so black, Joe had at first thought the man must wear contact lenses. Nwali wasn't the kind of man to wear contact lenses, though, he'd discovered in the last two weeks. In that time Nwali had not spoken a single word more than was absolutely necessary, had not allowed any deviations from or questions about his orders, whether they concerned cleaning the massive supply of firearms the group had or cooking dinner. He was their leader, a frugal, hard man who lived by a demanding, Spartan code.

He was also crazy, Joe had decided, a man who should be locked up someplace by himself for a long, long time.

"I thought I told you to wait inside by the entrance, Joseph," Nwali said.

"I was tired of getting shoved aside by Indonesian housewives with shopping lists. Then I ran into this woman," Joe said, turning to Endang.

She was gone. He scanned the crowd quickly, but she was nowhere in sight.

"That's funny," Joe said. "She was here a minute ago. Anyway, she gave me this." He handed Nwali the yellow handbill.

The man studied the piece of paper. *"Wayang kulit?"* He sounded amused. Then, for the first time since Joe had met him, Nwali smiled.

"You know what it is?" Joe asked.

Nwali gave the handbill back to Joe. "Yes."

"She seemed to think it would be worth seeing," Joe offered.

"You're not here as a tourist," Boris said harshly.

To Joe's surprise, Nwali disagreed. "Everyone should see a *wayang* performance at least once. It is the ultimate expression of Indonesian culture. I haven't seen one myself in years." The Assassin leader clapped a hand on Joe's shoulder, and Joe had to repress an instinctive shudder.

"But for now we have work to do."

If I'm going to do this, Frank Hardy thought, it has to be now, while I'm alone.

He brushed a strand of dark hair out of his eyes, and knelt next to the locked door. Then he jammed the small piece of metal into the keyhole and twisted the knob with his left hand, trying to get the tumblers to fall into place. The piece of metal was an old fishhook he'd found lying on the floor of the ship's engine room. He'd spent almost an hour bending it into a shape he could use.

Frank had wanted to get into this cabin since the first night he and Joe had been brought there from their late-night flight into Djakarta from Hawaii. They'd been whisked by van and then motorboat to this ship, an old frieghter called the *Hatta,* moored a few hundred feet off Djakarta's busy waterfront.

After they'd been shown to their bunks in a forward cabin Frank had been too keyed up to sleep. He'd wandered out to get a drink of water from the galley when he was stopped by the sound of voices. Curious, he'd followed the sound and found the door to this cabin open.

Nwali and Bob were inside, seated before a computer, pointing at the monitor and arguing. On the screen was an image of a mountain with a series of colorful Chinese pagodalike structures in front of it. He also saw a modem and a shortwave radio next to the computer. When Nwali turned and saw Frank the expression in his eyes had been almost lifeless and flat, but truly terrifying.

"Never come in this room again. Never," Nwali had intoned. Frank knew that if Nwali caught him breaking that command, he'd kill him.

That had been the most important incident to occur during their two-week stay in Djakarta until this morning, when Nwali had announced they would go into town for supplies.

Frank and Joe had spent the past two weeks playing endless card games and talking. In all that time none of the Assassins had uttered a single word about their mission. Clearly, they were waiting for someone to come or for something to happen.

Frank guessed that the Assassins were planning to do something with Dr. Stavrogin's equations. But what? Sell them to the highest bidder? A lot of countries would be willing to pay top dollar, and the thought of some of the world's dictatorships getting their hands on a nuclear bomb terrified Frank.

He wished he'd had more of a chance to talk to the Gray Man before they left Alaska. The Gray Man was high up in the Network and had helped the Hardys infiltrate the terrorist group.

Frank was sure the Gray Man hadn't told him and Joe everything. He remembered the tension in the man's voice when Frank mentioned that a certain Krinski now had Stavrogin's equations. The Gray Man had sounded panicked—and his reaction scared Frank.

Since they'd left Alaska Frank hadn't heard anything from the Gray Man or from the Network. So when Nwali had suddenly announced that they were going into town for supplies, Frank pretended to be sick. That left him alone on board with a chance to break into the cabin he now knelt in front of.

All at once the lock mechanism gave, and the door clicked once and popped open. Frank slipped silently inside.

A pale shaft of yellow light was coming through the cabin's lone porthole, but the brightest thing in the room was the blinking green cursor on the computer screen. He smiled to himself as he let his eyes adjust to the darkness. They'd left the system on. That made his job a lot easier.

Now the other objects before him were taking shape. Shortwave radio. Cellular phone. He stepped forward and lowered himself into the chair before the computer, his fingers poised above the keyboard. He was going to try to contact the Network.

Frank didn't like breaking procedure, but he wanted at least to let them know where he and

Joe had ended up. He planned to log on to a computer network and leave a coded message for the Gray Man. Maybe then Frank could ask some of the questions that had been bothering him for the past two weeks.

Before Frank could hit the first key, though, he heard wood creak behind him. Could they be back so soon? Frank spun around in his chair.

"What are you doing here?" The Assassin named Butch was standing in the doorway, glaring at him.

"The door was open," Frank said.

"You lie. The door was locked. It's always locked." The man held a ring of keys, which he quickly shoved into his pocket.

"Answer me, Hardy," Butch said, stepping forward. Jammed in the leather belt around his waist was a knife. "What," he said, reaching for the knife, "are you doing here?"

Chapter

2

"IT'S ABOUT TIME you got here," Bill said. He was leaning against the side of the beat-up old cargo van they had taken into town earlier that morning. As he talked he popped a handful of peanuts into his mouth and then tossed the shells into the gutter. He'd been eating peanuts night and day for two weeks and showed no sign of stopping.

Joe smiled wearily. "Long lines at the store."

The sliding door on the side of the van was open. Joe set down his bags and tried to wipe his forehead. His T-shirt was so soaked that it did no good.

Boris set his bags down next to Joe's. The big man didn't seem to be bothered by the heat.

"I have good news," Bill said, straightening

up and stretching. He was wearing military khakis, and he, at least, looked as sweaty as Joe felt. "Krinski's back. We can finally get this operation going."

Joe's heartbeat tripled.

"And there's still no sign of any Network agents," Bill added.

"*Bahasa,*" Nwali interrupted, raising a hand. Bill glanced at Joe and resumed speaking, but in what Joe knew was Indonesian.

Joe listened helplessly. There was something they didn't want him to know about.

"Hold on," Joe blurted out. "If this is about the Network, they killed my friend, remember? I've got as much right to know what's going on as anybody else."

Boris put a hand on his shoulder. A very big hand.

"You've got the rights we give to you," he said.

"I didn't join the organization to carry groceries." Joe picked up Boris's hand and removed it from his shoulder. "I want to know what's happening."

Boris grunted. Bill folded his arms across his chest. Both turned to Nwali, who stared at Joe for what seemed a full minute before speaking.

"Perhaps my comrades didn't explain the way our organization works when you were recruited," Nwali said finally. "Let me rectify that error."

Eau Claire District Library

He took a step forward so that he was within inches of Joe.

"You'll carry groceries for the rest of this mission if we decide that is what we need you to do. We will decide what you have a right to know, and when. You, in turn, will follow our orders exactly. Is that clear?"

"Yes," Joe said, sensing Boris waiting and ready for action. These guys would kill him if he gave them much more trouble. "But I want you to know I'm not in this for the money. I want to nail the people who killed Gina."

"Of course," Nwali said. "For now, though, you do as you're told."

Right, Joe added silently. Until Frank and I find out what you're up to. Then you belong to the Network.

Nwali climbed into the front passenger seat while Joe and Boris settled themselves in the rear among the supplies.

So Krinski's arrival was what they'd been waiting for the past two weeks. Now all he and Frank had to figure out was who Krinski was, and where he and the Assassins planned to sell Stavrogin's equations.

The van pulled out into traffic just as a horse-drawn cart pulled out of a side street ahead of them.

Bill honked the horn loudly. "Move that thing!"

The cart's driver, an elderly man in a colorful, patterned shirt, turned and smiled at Bill. His passengers, a bearded man and a blond woman, glared at the van momentarily, then resumed talking to each other. Judging from the clothes, Joe figured the man and woman were tourists.

"It's going to take us twenty minutes to go a block at this rate," Bill said, shaking his head. "Why do they still permit those things on the street?"

"They look kind of cool," Joe said.

"Cool?" Nwali asked, turning to him. "As in quaint?" He sounded angry. "Look at these people."

Joe looked. They were driving down a large avenue now, and one entire side of the street was filled with small stalls, with merchants selling native handicrafts of every kind. There was even a group of dancers in a small space between two stalls.

"Hawking their traditions, their very beliefs, older by a thousand years than those of the West, for the almighty dollar. It disgusts me," Nwali said, shaking his head.

Joe didn't know what to say, and he certainly didn't want to get Nwali any angrier at him, so he kept his mouth shut.

"All this has to change," Nwali said. "And it will, soon enough." The Assassin leader turned in his seat again and spent the rest of the ride back to the waterfront in silence.

Joe was also quiet as he tried to figure out what Nwali's cryptic last words had meant.

"Move away from the keyboard, Hardy," Butch said, drawing his knife.

"Take it easy," Frank said, standing and stepping back. "Like I said, the door was open."

"Don't waste your breath," Butch said curtly. "Now turn around."

Frank complied, his mind racing as the Assassin checked him for weapons. No matter what kind of explanation he came up with for being in the room, Nwali wasn't going to buy it. That meant he and Joe were dead men. He had to get off the ship and warn his brother. There was an American embassy in Djakarta; if the two of them could make it there, they'd be safe.

"Do you really think Nwali would trust you here all alone?" Butch said. "No. While the others went to town and Bob went to check on his helicopter, I stayed here to keep an eye on you, and look what I found. Now move," Butch continued. "Out on deck."

Frank felt the sharp point of the knife digging into the small of his back as Butch shoved him out of the cabin, which he locked. Frank had to shield his eyes when he went up on deck. The sun was directly overhead and unbelievably bright. He felt the pressure in Butch's knife hand ease up just a fraction. He must have been blinded by the sun, too.

Frank spun at that moment and grabbed the Assassin's wrist with both hands.

"You fool," Butch said, struggling to break his grip. "I'll kill you."

"Why not drop the knife instead?" Frank said. He let go of the Assassin's wrist with his right hand and drove his right fist straight into Butch's stomach. He heard the man gasp and brought his left knee up into Butch's knife hand. The weapon clattered to the deck.

They dived after it at exactly the same time. Frank got there first, grabbed the knife, and somersaulted away from Butch. When he turned back to face him, Butch was standing motionless, staring at him.

"You're dead, Hardy," Butch said. "Nwali will kill you when he returns. Or perhaps he'll give you to Boris."

Frank felt the deck railing at his back. For a second he considered jumping overboard and swimming for shore, but that would mean leaving Joe to these creeps.

"Why don't you use that knife, boy?" Butch taunted, circling him. "Or don't you know how?"

"I know how," Frank said, unsure that he could, even if it came down to his life versus Butch's.

Butch must have read the hesitation in his

eyes. The man charged him, ducking under the knife, and tackled him. Frank fell back, crashing into the wooden handrail that circled the ship.

There was a loud crack. The next second the two of them were hurtling through the air, heading for the ocean below!

Chapter

3

FRANK FELT Butch's grip loosen and fall away. A split second later he slammed into the ocean. At almost the same time he heard Butch hit the water next to him.

Before he knew what was happening Frank felt the Assassin's hands on his arm. He was trying to get the knife away from Frank.

"Not so fast," Frank said. He raised his right knee up to his chin and then thrust it forward, catching the man in the chest. The blow caught Butch just right and knocked him back.

Butch recovered and lunged for him again. This time Frank wasn't quick enough to escape, and Butch forced his head underwater with one hand. He ripped the knife out of Frank's grasp with the other.

Frank was desperate to free himself—he couldn't breathe. Everything was happening in slow motion. Butch's knife slid through the water next to Frank. Frank kicked away, and the knife missed his shoulder by inches.

"Hold still!" Butch yelled. He seemed to be moving at half speed, too. Fighting in the water was tiring both of them. The Assassin had the edge, though. He was willing to kill, and Frank wasn't.

Frank kicked and shot upward so his head could break the surface. Gasping for air, he looked toward the waterfront. It was half a mile away.

Even though he was exhausted, he forced himself to swim in the direction of the docks. It was his only way out. Ignoring the tightness in his lungs and the pounding of his heart, Frank pulled with all his strength.

The next thing he knew, he was touching wood. A dock. He broke the surface and looked around. There was the motorboat that had ferried him and Joe to the *Hatta* that first night. He pulled himself up onto the planking.

Suddenly agony erupted along the back of his right leg.

He fell backward into the ocean. Butch, just a few feet behind him, had slashed him with the knife!

"Let's see you swim now," the Assassin said, his mouth twisted in a cruel imitation of a smile.

Then all at once Butch screamed.

Frank didn't know what had happened. Then he saw a flash of gray and black stripes slither past him. Frank shuddered. It was a snake.

"Help me," Butch cried out. He dropped the knife and turned back toward the dock.

"Easy," Frank said. He swam up beside him and gave the Assassin a boost up onto the dock. As he did so a thick white plastic card fell out of Butch's pocket. Frank grabbed it and shoved it in his own pocket.

He pulled himself up on the dock and helped Butch lie down. The man was hyperventilating now, and on his right leg a nasty-looking bruise was beginning to swell. Whatever kind of snake had bitten him must have been poisonous.

"Take it easy," Frank said. "We'll get a doctor."

Butch convulsed once, then clutched Frank's shirt with a hand. His eyes glazed over. Frank touched the side of his neck. No pulse, nothing. The man was dead.

"What's happening?"

Frank turned.

Joe was standing on the pier above him, looking down. Next to him, eyes fixed on Frank, was Nwali.

"You're sure you're okay?" Joe asked.

"Fine," Frank said, checking the slash on the back of his leg. "The cut's not that deep."

21

He and Joe were sitting side by side on their bottom bunk. The bed took up most of their small cabin. The only other furniture was a small built-in dresser with three drawers and a tiny mirror screwed to the wall just above it. It wasn't much, but right then Frank felt lucky to have it.

The alternative would be a spot on the floor of the Assassins' van, where Butch was right now. Boris was taking his fallen comrade's body to be buried. If not for that snake, Frank and Joe would be sharing that spot on the van's floor.

"I think Nwali bought your explanation," Joe said.

Frank shook his head. "I'm not so sure." He'd told the Assassins' leader that he and Butch had been roughhousing on deck and fell against the rail, which broke. The two had fallen into the ocean, where Butch had been bitten by a snake. An accident, pure and simple.

Nwali hadn't asked a single question when Frank finished telling his story. He'd just nodded his head and then had Joe escort Frank back to their cabin.

"How much worse off could we be, anyway?" Joe asked. "It's not like they tell us what's going on now."

"That's true," Frank admitted. "We still don't know what we've been waiting for for the past two weeks or who this mysterious Krinski is."

"I think we'll be finding out soon enough," Joe said.

"Oh?" Frank turned to Joe, who had a half smile on his face. "And why is that?"

"Because he's here."

"What?" Frank asked excitedly. "You saw him?"

"Take it easy," Joe said. "No, I didn't see him, but Bill said he'd arrived." With that he told Frank everything that had happened to him that day, starting with his run-in with Endang.

"I almost forgot," Frank said when he finished. He pulled out Butch's thick white plastic card from his pocket and handed it to Joe. "What do you make of this?"

"It looks like one of those magnetic ID cards," Joe said. He turned it over. Both sides were completely blank. "Where'd you get it?"

"From Butch, before he died." Frank took the card and slipped it back in his pocket. "Keep an eye out for where we might use it."

Joe nodded just as the door to their cabin swung open.

"All right, you two, out on deck," Bill said, stepping inside and focusing on Joe. "You wanted to do something besides carry groceries, here's your chance."

"Really? What's up?" Joe asked.

Bill smiled. "Come topside and you'll see."

They followed him up on deck to find another

ship pulled up near them. The newcomer was an unmarked freighter, all rusted metal and peeling gray paint, slightly larger than theirs. A small crane set in the middle of the second ship was lowering crates directly into the *Hatta*'s cargo hold.

"Break for a minute!" Bill yelled across to the man operating the crane. He turned back to the Hardys. "I want you two to go below and stack those crates. Make sure we're not unbalanced."

He pointed to the top of a metal ladder poking out of the hold. "You climb down over there. When you're done give a yell up, and we'll send more crates down."

"I think we can handle that," Joe said. Without another word he disappeared down the ladder. Frank followed him into the freighter's dim, musty cargo hold.

"Whoa, it stinks in here," Joe said, holding his nose. "This must be Boris's room."

"Very funny," Frank said. The hold was only about six feet high, so he knew he'd have to crouch down to move about. As he stepped off the ladder he did bump his head on the single source of light, one bulb dangling from a fraying electric wire. The bouncing bulb cast strange shadows on either side of him, like those from a strobe light.

Frank quickly counted a half dozen crates scattered about the hold, with "SMCS" stenciled on them in letters about six inches high. Each crate was approximately the size of an old steamer trunk.

"Let's stack three on each side," Frank said, taking hold of one crate and sliding it toward him. "Grab the other end."

"Aren't you forgetting something?" Joe asked. "Don't we want to see what's inside these crates?"

"Of course," Frank answered quietly. He glanced upward. "But let's make a little noise for our friend up there first. Let him think we're hard at work." He set the crate down and slid it flush against the hold's side, letting it drag against the ground so that it made a huge scraping sound. "What do you think these initials stand for?"

Joe shook his head. "I don't know. Maybe that's what's in them, something called SMCS. There's only one way to find out for sure, though."

The lid of the crate was nailed shut. Frank came up with a crowbar discarded in a corner. He jammed it into the space between the lid and the edge of the crate and ran the bar around the edge of the crate several times. He was able to pry the top up gradually without bending the nails, and finally the lid came off.

To Frank's surprise, the crate was filled with construction hard hats.

"I don't get this," Frank said, shoving the lid

back on the crate. He and Joe quickly pushed the nails back into place. "Let's try another."

"Hurry it up down there!" Bill shouted down. "What's taking you so long?"

"We're almost done!" Frank yelled back.

Joe had moved to another crate that had red Indonesian writing stenciled across it. He was busy prying off its lid. He was faster at it than Frank had been.

"Want to bet the lunch pails are in this one?" he asked as the lid lifted up with a screech.

Frank reached around Joe and dug his hand into the crate. "It's straw," he said, pulling out a handful. "It must be covering something."

He dug in deeper, and his fingers touched metal. Carefully he pulled out an oblong metal framework about the size of a milk crate.

"What's this?" Frank asked, holding it up to the light. He spun it around in his hand and studied it from every angle. It looked almost like some sort of helmet, but the space inside was barely big enough for a child's head.

Then the realization hit him.

"You look sick," Joe said. "What's the matter?"

"I feel sick," Frank replied. He held out the lattice of metal for his brother to examine. "You know what this is?"

Joe shook his head. "From the tone of your voice, I'll bet it's not a lunch pail."

"You can say that again. What we have here," Frank said quietly, "is part of the reaction chamber for a hydrogen bomb. This"—he pointed to the empty space in the center—"is where the plutonium goes."

For once Joe was speechless.

"The Assassins don't plan on selling Stavrogin's formula to anyone," Frank said. "They're going to build a hydrogen bomb themselves."

Chapter
4

JOE SAT DOWN heavily on top of another crate. Frank's words were spinning in his head—the Assassins were building a hydrogen bomb. "What do you think they plan to do with it?" he asked.

"What do terrorists do with any weapon?" Frank shook his head. "Kill people." His voice sounded detached, as if he couldn't believe what he was saying.

Joe couldn't believe it, either. For the first time in his life he felt he was involved in something way over his head. They weren't just solving a simple mystery here. They were dealing with lunatics who would have the means to murder millions of people.

"We have to get to the Gray Man," Joe said.

"That's for sure," Frank agreed. "But we've got to finish stacking these crates first."

Joe got to his feet as his brother replaced the metal framework in the crate. He helped Frank seal it shut.

"All set down here!" Frank yelled up. While they waited for the crane to send down the rest of the crates he turned back to his brother.

"Got any ideas on how to contact the Network?" Frank asked. "It's not like these guys are going to let us off the ship."

Joe thought a minute. "Maybe," he said. "It depends on how culturally deprived our leader is feeling."

"It has been fifteen years since I've seen *wayang*," Nwali said. The Assassin leader paused a moment before dipping a shrimp cracker in the red sauce before him. He used his right hand, of course. He'd told Frank and Joe the left was considered unclean by Indonesians, especially on his home island of Bali. "I fear the art will have decayed in this much time."

The sauce was *sambal,* red chili paste—a condiment Indonesians used on their food the way Americans used salt. Frank had tried some earlier, but a pinch of it had taken off the top layer of skin on his tongue.

Nwali swallowed a teaspoonful with a smile.

"I hope not," Frank said. "You make it sound interesting."

Nwali had explained something of the *wayang kulit* during their meal. It sounded like puppet theater to Frank, only more complicated. The *dalang* was the puppet master, responsible for the movements and voices of up to hundreds of different puppets. The audience actually saw only the shadow of the puppet. It was projected onto a screen that the *dalang* sat behind.

It really did sound interesting, but right then the only thing Frank could think of was the cargo in the *Hatta*'s hold.

He still didn't know why Nwali had agreed to Joe's suggestion that they see the *wayang* performance. The Assassin leader had even treated them to a meal in a small restaurant on the outskirts of Djakarta. Maybe he was celebrating the arrival of those crates. Or the mysterious Dr. Krinski. Or maybe, as Joe had suggested, he had gotten tired of nothing but tea and grapefruit.

Frank wasn't about to complain. The meal was easily the best food he'd had in a month. Nwali had called the food *rijstafel,* "rice table." The dish got its name from the huge bowl of rice the waiter set in the middle of the table. A half dozen other dishes came with it. Those were on a separate serving platter, each in its own small metal dish.

"Try this one," Nwali said, pushing the serving platter toward Frank. *"Daging bakar pelecing."* The dish facing him had pieces of what

30

looked like steak, with little flecks of red pepper on the surface. Frank hoped the flakes weren't as hot as the *sambal*.

He cut off a small piece of the meat and popped it in his mouth with some rice.

"Wow," he said. "That's great."

Nwali almost smiled. "Some of our traditions, at least, remain unchanged. But the *wayang* will have decayed," he repeated. "Forty years ago there were thousands of *dalang*s on Bali. Today there are perhaps a hundred. The influx of Western culture, the lure of money, a faster-paced life-style—all have combined to destroy our traditions. Americans," he said, focusing on Frank, "are mainly to blame."

The conversation, which had been lively until Nwali's accusation, came to an abrupt halt. The rest of the meal passed in silence. After dessert the three took a taxi to the arts center.

Stepping out of the cab, Joe got caught up in the middle of a group of tourists lined up to buy snack cakes and drinks outside the center. He stopped for a minute to take a look at the building.

All concrete and steel, the TIM looked like it could have been plopped down in any city, anywhere in the world. There was nothing Indonesian about it at all. For a split second Joe sympathized with Nwali's earlier ravings about how native traditions were disappearing. Then he remembered the man was a lunatic.

Nwali led them inside the auditorium, where several hundred people were milling around, none of whom seemed in a hurry to take their seats. On the stage a transparent white screen about six feet high by twelve feet across had been set up between two metal rods. A light bulb shone through the screen from behind.

"In front," Nwali said, pointing toward the stage. "We'll get the best view of the *dalang* from there."

He led them to the right-hand side of the theater. From where they sat Joe could see behind the screen by leaning forward. Several dozen incredibly detailed puppets, made of leather and decorated with jewels, hung from supports on either side of the screen. There was a large cushioned seat directly behind it. For the *dalang,* he guessed.

"Joe!"

He turned. Endang was standing in the aisle next to him, smiling.

"I'm glad to see you could make it," she said.

"Who is this, Joseph?" Nwali asked, his eyes never leaving Endang's face.

"Endang. She's the girl I met at the supermarket, who told me about the *wayang*." He smiled at her and stood. "This is my brother, Frank, and our host—"

"Pleased to meet you," Nwali said, interrupting the introduction.

Endang nodded in greeting. "Do you have a

minute?" she asked Joe. "There are some friends I'd like you to meet."

"Sure," he said. This was a real break. Now he wouldn't even have to make up an excuse to get away. "I'll be right back."

He followed Endang as she pushed her way through the crowd toward the back of the auditorium.

"Are these shows always this jammed?" he called after her.

She turned and nodded. "This way," she said, taking his arm and leading him through an unmarked door. It shut behind him, and suddenly the crowd noise disappeared entirely.

"Hey," Joe asked. "Where are we going?"

"I told you, there are some people I need you to meet."

"Hold on a second," Joe said, pulling free of her grasp.

"Right in here, Joe," she persisted. They came to another door, which she pushed open. "Here are my friends."

Reluctantly Joe stepped inside.

The room was bare except for a small folding table with two men seated around it. One man, who looked like an American, was wearing a dark suit, white shirt, and dark blue tie. Joe would have pegged him as FBI, except this was Indonesia. Even sitting, he was big, probably well over six feet tall, and close to two hundred and fifty pounds.

The other man was clearly an Indonesian, short, solidly built, with a round face and golden brown skin. He was wearing a military uniform.

"This is the man?" the Indonesian asked. "He looks so young."

She nodded. "This is Joe Hardy."

"Good," the man in the dark suit said, standing now. His suit coat was open, and Joe caught a glimpse of a shoulder holster with a gun in it. "We have a lot of questions for you."

Chapter
5

FRANK WAS GETTING WORRIED. Fifteen minutes had passed, and Joe still hadn't returned.

He wasn't worried about his brother's safety. He suspected Joe had gotten away from Endang and was busy trying to contact the Network. He was worried that Nwali was going to get suspicious.

He watched the Assassin leader, who was intently studying the preparations on the stage.

"You must forgive my preoccupation," Nwali said. He sounded different, almost nostalgic. "This is all so familiar, and yet so very, very different. The size of this auditorium, all those microphones, and a light bulb . . ." Nwali's voice trailed off. He shook his head. "The corruption of the form," he said almost to himself.

35

Frank followed Nwali's gaze to the stage. The microphones he was talking about hung suspended over the *dalang*'s throne, and the light bulbs illuminated the screen from behind.

"Those are just technological improvements, though," Frank said. "They don't change what's in the performance."

"Ah, I think you are wrong," Nwali said. "You see, my father was a *dalang*. I was going to be one, too." He fell silent again, lost in thought.

Frank wanted to know why Nwali hadn't followed in his father's footsteps, but he didn't want to disturb him while he was deep in thought. At least the man wasn't worrying about where Joe was.

Almost as if he were reading Frank's mind, Nwali abruptly stood. "I think I will go and see what is keeping your brother," he said. "After all, we would not want him to miss the start of the performance."

"Remember the agreement, Ali," Endang said, circling the table. "I'm in charge here. I'll ask the questions."

Joe was confused. "What questions? What are you two talking about?"

"We followed you here to Djakarta."

He shook his head, still not getting it. "We?"

"Yes, we." Endang smiled. "I'm with the Network."

Joe wasn't about to blow the cover that he and Frank had worked so hard to establish. "What network?" he asked. "What are you talking about?"

"Don't be stupid," Endang said. There was a strength in her voice that hadn't been there a moment ago. Joe thought she seemed about a dozen years older. Even if she wasn't a Network agent, she was clearly not a young and innocent girl.

Endang leaned against the table, staring directly at Joe. "We've only got a few minutes before your friends get suspicious and come after you, and there's a lot I need to tell you. And a lot I want to hear from you."

Joe folded his arms. "I don't know who you are."

"Hey, look, kid." The man dressed like an FBI agent stepped forward now and pointed a finger at Joe. "You may not be in the chain of command, but I can have your—"

"Take it easy, Mike," Endang said. She laid a hand across the man's chest. "Keep a lookout, will you?"

The man nodded and stepped out of the room, quietly shutting the door behind him.

"All right, Joe," she began again. "You don't believe I'm with the Network. Then how about this?" She handed him a silver-colored diamond-shaped tag.

Joe's eyes widened involuntarily. That was what had started it all, almost a month earlier—

the luggage tags that the theft ring had been using to mark items at the Atlanta airport.

Still, just because she had the tag didn't mean she was with the Network. She could be one of the thieves, even an Assassin herself, putting Joe's loyalty to yet another test.

"Show me something else," he commanded.

"Why don't I tell you something?" Endang said. "Like the last words the Gray Man said before you left Alaska two weeks ago: 'This could be much worse than we feared.' "

Joe nodded. "Close enough," he said. "How did you find me? And why haven't you contacted us sooner?"

"There hasn't been a chance," Endang replied. "I've been watching you, and the Assassins haven't left you alone until today. As for how we found you, one of our men spotted an Assassin landing at Djakarta two weeks ago. In fact, it was special agent Michael Thomas, the man keeping a lookout in the corridor now. By the way, this is Colonel Ali Mangkupradja," she said. "He's our liaison with the Indonesian government."

Joe nodded. Considering the stakes involved here, the Network would have a hard time keeping this affair entirely secret from the local authorities.

"Now," she said, sitting down at the table, "I want you to tell me everything you've found out over the last two weeks."

"There's only one thing you really need to know," Joe said. He took a deep breath. "In the hold of the *Hatta* are several crates. We found a metal casing in one that my brother thinks is part of a hydrogen bomb."

"My god," Colonel Mangkupradja said, sitting down next to Endang.

"Continue," Endang said.

Joe told her other things that had happened to him and Frank, and he'd just gotten to that day's events, with the news of Krinski's arrival, when Thomas came back into the room.

"The man you came in with is heading this way," Thomas said. "Looking for you."

Endang nodded. "Colonel, you and Agent Thomas stay here. Come on, Joe," she said, taking his hand and leading him out into the corridor. Joe heard the footsteps coming just as Endang shut the door.

"We'll pretend we've just been standing here talking," she said.

Joe shook his head. "Who's going to believe that? I've got a better idea," he said.

Before Endang could do anything he bent down and kissed her just as Nwali rounded the corner.

"Joseph," he said with a frown. "Your energy is admirable, but you're about to miss the performance."

"Right," Joe said. "Give me one more minute."

Nwali left.

"That worked pretty well," Joe said, smiling at Endang. "Don't you think?"

"I'm a third-degree black belt," she said quietly. "You try that again, and I'll break your arm."

"It was the best I could do on such short notice," Joe said. "Now listen. You've got to answer some questions for me. Who's this Krinski the Gray Man was so scared of? Why is his arrival such a big deal?"

In answer Endang reached into her handbag to take out a snapshot. She handed it to Joe. It showed a young man with frizzy red hair, probably in his early twenties, standing in front of a blackboard. He was wearing a Dallas Cowboys sweatshirt with the number twelve on it. An older, gray-haired man stood next to him, holding a pointer in one hand. His other hand rested on top of the young man's shoulder.

"Hey," Joe said. "The older guy, that's Dr. Stavrogin. He's the one whose equations the Assassins stole."

"Krinski is the younger one," Endang added. "They worked together one summer at MIT. Krinski's a prodigy who defected from Romania when he was twelve so he could work with Stavrogin. He finished college at fourteen, grad school at twenty. You two should get along famously."

"Oh?" Joe asked. "Why is that?"

"Because he loves anything and everything to

do with America. And you definitely fit that category."

Joe handed her back the picture. "So why did the Gray Man become so panicked when he heard his name?"

"Because of the research he did with Stavrogin," she said. "In particular, a specific proposal they were working on, 'The Geophysical Application of Thermonuclear Devices.'"

"Huh?"

Endang smiled. "I'll put it in English for you. Using atomic explosives to reshape strategically critical areas."

Joe frowned. "I still don't get it."

"For example," she continued, "they proposed using a nuclear bomb to dig a new Panama Canal."

"What?" Joe said, so loud that his voice echoed in the empty corridor. "That's crazy!"

"Keep your voice down," Endang warned, shaking her head. "It's not a farfetched idea, not at all. The Panama Canal is so old that none of the new supertankers can use it. A sea-level canal, like the one Krinski was recommending, makes tremendous economic sense."

She leaned in closer and spoke more intently. "Listen, Joe, you have to understand something about Krinski. He achieved everything most people could by the time he was twenty. People like that, they just have to keep doing bigger and better things. When the U.S. government wouldn't go ahead with his project, Krinski decided to sell his expertise elsewhere.''

"To terrorists."

"It seems so," Endang replied. "Anyway, he's not in Indonesia to build a canal. He's here to build a hydrogen bomb."

"Can he do it?"

"If the Assassins can get him the materials, he's perfectly capable of constructing it." She frowned. "Although Indonesia's certainly not the first place I would have picked to put it together. The infrastructure just isn't here." Her frown deepened. "Now you'd better get back before Nwali comes looking for you again."

"At least we've got a way to contact each other again," Joe said. "That kiss. It gives you the perfect excuse to visit the *Hatta*."

"And what if you need to get in touch with me?" she asked.

"There's not much I can do about that," Joe said. "They've let us off the boat only twice in the last two weeks."

"All right." Endang nodded. "I'll be in touch. Good luck."

Joe walked back to his seat, still shaking his head. Build a new canal, as if you could rearrange the continents like Tinkertoys. What kind of nut thought like that? Krinski and Nwali probably made quite a team.

"Joe!"

He turned at the sound of his brother's voice.

He'd been so lost in thought he'd walked right by his seat.

Only it wasn't his seat anymore. There was someone else sitting in it now. Someone tall and lanky, with a mushroom cloud of frizzy red hair. Someone who looked remarkably like the young man in the picture Endang had shown him a few minutes earlier.

"You must be Joe Hardy," the newcomer said, standing. "I've heard a lot about you."

He held out his hand, and Joe took it, trying to mask his surprise.

"I'm Alex Krinski."

Chapter

6

"NOW THAT YOU'RE HERE," Krinski said, "we can go."

"Go?" Joe shook his head, confused. What was going on here?

Nwali stood. "Yes, we will go."

The tone of Nwali's voice left no doubt in Joe's mind. He wasn't about to argue. They were going.

They hurried out of the theater just as the *dalang* was walking onto the stage.

"There has been a slight change of plan," Nwali announced as soon as they were outside. "Professor Krinski requires our assistance."

Krinski nodded, turning to face Joe as he did so. "What are two young Americans like you and your brother doing with this group?"

Joe shrugged. "Making a lot of money, we hope."

Nwali came up behind Krinski and put a hand on his shoulder. Krinski flinched at the Assassin's touch.

"These are very practical young men, as I told you," Nwali said.

The Assassin leader hailed them a taxi. Joe crowded in front with the driver, who followed the directions Krinski gave him. About twenty minutes later the car turned into a long, circular drive lined with tall palms. They pulled up in front of a huge old mansion with white stone columns flanking the front entrance.

"Wow," Frank said. "What hotel is this?"

Krinski, next to him in the backseat, smiled. "This is no hotel. This is my house."

As Joe was climbing out he caught a glimpse of another building out back. It was surrounded by a high stone wall that made it impossible to see anything other than the roof.

"This guy's so rich, that's probably the doghouse," he whispered, falling back next to his brother.

Frank smiled. "Only if it's a very big dog."

Krinski stopped at the front door. Next to it was an oversize keypad with letters and numbers just like a phone. Joe heard him punch in five digits. With a barely audible click the door swung open.

"Welcome to my home." Krinski held the

door open to let the others pass through. The contrast in styles between the inside and outside of the house couldn't have been greater.

When Endang said Krinski was fascinated by America she wasn't kidding, Joe thought. A huge Dallas Cowboys poster hung on the wall directly opposite the entranceway. A photo of Humphrey Bogart hung to the right. Every wall Joe could see was painted a different Day-Glo color. He couldn't believe the interior's contrast with the muted exterior.

To Joe's left was a pair of double doors. Krinski opened them, revealing a living room with an entertainment center that looked as if it belonged on display in a state-of-the-art electronics store.

An enormous projection TV screen dominated the room. Two leather couches were arranged in an L shape in front of it. Next to the television was an elaborate stereo and CD system. In the far corner was a mainframe computer flanked by two terminals.

"Susanto!" Krinski called.

A young woman appeared in an arched entranceway on the far side of the room and smiled at Krinski expectantly. She had long blond hair with golden tan skin and was dressed in a checkered miniskirt.

"Snacks," Krinski commanded the young woman.

Susanto nodded and returned minutes later

with a pot of steaming hot tea and a plate of American cookies—Oreos, Fig Newtons, and chocolate-covered graham crackers. She set them down on the coffee table, and Joe scooped up a handful. He almost inhaled the cookies, he was so glad to see familiar food.

"This is quite a collection you have here, Professor," Joe heard his brother say. Frank was standing next to a cabinet filled floor to ceiling with videocassettes. "You like gangster movies, I see."

Krinski nodded. "Especially the ones with Humphrey Bogart. I have all of them. In fact, I had one on this morning while the simulations were running." He picked up a remote control and pressed a button. The TV screen flared to life.

"I'm sure this is a fascinating film," Nwali said. "But in light of the work we must do, perhaps we can watch it some other time."

The doorbell rang.

Krinski pressed another button on the remote control, and the image on the screen changed to reveal Bob standing at the door. Behind him in the driveway was a huge tractor-trailer.

Joe knew why Nwali had agreed to take him and Frank to the *wayang* performance that night. The other Assassins had been busy with things they didn't want the Hardys to know about.

47

"Let's go," Nwali said, smiling directly at Joe. "Time to move some more groceries."

"What's in here? Lead weights?" Frank asked, setting his end of a crate down on a waiting dolly. The truck they were unloading was filled with more crates, all identical to those they'd unloaded onto the *Hatta* earlier in the day but far heavier.

"One thing's for sure," Joe replied, stopping to catch his breath. "It isn't groceries."

These crates had SMCS stenciled on the side, too, Frank noticed. Krinski had instructed them to put two on a dolly and bring them around back to the building behind the house. Bob had already wheeled the first load away.

"Come on," Frank said, grabbing hold of one of the two dollies. "Let's catch up." He was anxious to see what was inside the other building.

Joe took the other dolly and pushed it up onto the narrow concrete walk that led around to the back of the house. As they cleared the back of the mansion Frank took a glance around. No one else was in earshot.

"Did you get through to our friends before?" he asked quietly.

"Did I ever," Joe said, nodding. He finished filling in Frank on the details as they moved up alongside Bob. The Assassin pilot had stopped next to a huge metal gate set directly into the concrete wall before them. The wall ran all the way around the building; the gate in front of them was the only way in. There was a keypad beside it.

"I don't know the code," Bob said, obviously irritated. "We'll have to wait."

Half a minute later Krinski strolled up the path and punched in the code. To Frank it sounded like the same five-digit sequence as before.

"This way," Krinski said, pushing open the gate. To Frank's surprise, the stone wall extended on both sides to the actual front door of the building, forming a corridor for them to walk down.

The door into the building swung open at Krinski's touch. Frank wheeled his dolly after the professor, following him into a large, featureless room with concrete floors and high ceilings. On the opposite side of the room was an oversize dull gray metal door. Frank was eager to know what was behind it.

Krinski had them unload the crates in the middle of the floor and then return for more. It took almost an hour to unload the truck. Halfway through the job Boris and Bill showed up, which was good. The last few crates were so heavy that all five of them were needed to move just one. Frank was hoping Krinski would unseal a crate, but he just had them stack the crates in as compact a pile as possible.

When they were done they returned to the house and discovered that Nwali had left for the *Hatta*. The five of them were to spend the night at Krinski's.

After Krinski showed the Hardys to the room they were sharing and said good night, Frank turned to Joe and put a finger to his lips. He mouthed the word *bugged*. He wasn't positive someone would be listening in, but with all the high-tech electronics Krinski had, he was taking no chances.

"I want to take a shower before we hit the sack," he said, a little louder than he had to. "We'll probably have to get an early start tomorrow." He motioned for Joe to follow him into the bathroom.

After turning on the water, he said, "We can talk now."

"What do you think's going on?" Joe asked.

"Building a hydrogen bomb is delicate work. Not the kind of thing that could be done on a boat that rolls with the waves. My guess is they're assembling the bomb here, in that building out back." He frowned. "This could be our chance—maybe our only chance. Let's give them time to fall asleep and then do a little exploring."

For the next hour Frank lay silently in the darkness, waiting. Finally he sat up, reached over, and shook Joe awake. His brother's eyes popped open, and he sat up, too.

They tiptoed barefoot out into the hall and down the stairs. Frank stopped at the keypad by the front door. A red light on it was blinking.

"Wait a minute," Joe whispered. "He's got this entire place armed. If we go outside, we'll set off the alarm. How are we even going to get outside?"

Frank smiled. "I know the code," he said.

"How?" Joe asked. "Did you look over his shoulder?"

Frank shook his head.

"You heard the tones the numbers made?"

Frank shook his head. "Come on. He practically gave it to us when we walked in."

"I must have been sleeping," Joe said. "What is it?"

Frank pointed over his shoulder at the picture of Humphrey Bogart on the wall.

"B-O-G-E-Y," he said.

Joe's eyes widened in fear. "You're just guessing."

"It's an educated guess," Frank replied.

"I hope it's right," Joe said. "Otherwise we're going to have to do some very quick explaining."

"Forget the explaining," Frank said, leaning over the keypad. "We're going to have to do some very quick running." He took a deep breath. "Here goes nothing."

Frank punched in the numbers. The red light went off, and the door swung open.

He turned to Joe and smiled. "After you."

They moved to the back of the mansion and across the moonlit yard to the cinder-block building. Frank punched in the same code on the keypad there.

"Easy as pie," he said, pushing the metal gate open. As he walked toward the front door he wondered again why the wall circling the building sealed the path off from the rest of the yard. It was as if there was something behind those walls Krinski didn't want anyone to see. Frank didn't much care—he was interested in what was in the building, not what was outside of it.

When he reached the front door it was shut.

"Locked," Frank said disgustedly, trying the knob. "Krinski's probably got the only key."

Joe tapped him on the shoulder. "Hey," he said, pointing up at the concrete wall. "We could climb over. Maybe there's a window around the back we can get in through."

Frank nodded reluctantly. "Krinski doesn't seem like the kind of guy to leave anything unlocked, but at this point it may be our best shot."

Joe nodded. "Let's do it."

Frank cupped his hands and gave Joe a boost so he could reach the top of the wall and pull himself up onto it. Joe lay flat on top of the wall and stretched a hand down to Frank, who was just able to reach it and pull himself up.

Frank stared down at the yard below. It was

almost completely empty, except for a stone sculpture of a small dinosaur at one end, away from the building.

"Feel the inside of the wall," Joe said to him. "It's smooth as glass."

He leaned over the edge and rubbed it. "You're right. It's a completely different texture. But why?"

"I don't know about you, but I don't have time to figure it out," Joe said. Then, before Frank could say anything more, Joe jumped, somersaulting as he landed and rolling to his feet. He gave Frank the thumbs-up sign.

Frank shrugged and jumped, too, landing the same way his brother had.

"Now let's see if we can find a way in," Frank said. "Maybe around back—"

Joe's arm shot out like a clothesline across his brother's chest, stopping Frank dead in his tracks.

"Frank," he said, pointing across the yard. "I don't think that's a statue."

Sure enough, Frank saw the statue moving toward them.

"It's alive," Frank said, not believing his own words. He watched the creature move closer to them. It had to be at least eight feet long and weigh several hundred pounds. "It's a dinosaur, and it's alive!"

"Yeah," Joe said, backing up. "Let's just hope it's not hungry."

Chapter

7

"THAT'S NO DINOSAUR," Frank said suddenly as the creature moved closer. "It's a Komodo dragon!"

Joe swallowed hard. He had once read about Komodo dragons in *National Geographic*. "They're man-eaters, aren't they?"

"They can be," Frank said.

The creature flicked a forked tongue at them and took another step forward.

Joe reacted by taking another step back. "This proves Krinski's crazy," he said. "What kind of lunatic has a Komodo dragon for a watchdog?"

As if it knew they were talking about it, the dragon hissed again and let out a low rumble from the base of its throat.

"Maybe we can run around it," Joe suggested. "It doesn't look fast."

"Run around it and do what? Dig a hole under the wall?" Frank shook his head. "Look at those claws. If that thing caught us, we'd be finished."

Frank was right. Each claw on the giant lizard's foot was at least six inches long.

"What do you suggest?" Joe asked.

"No sudden movements," Frank said, backing up against the wall. "We go out the way we came in." He cupped his hands together. "Come on. Jump up. Then you can pull me up."

"You go first," Joe said.

"This is no time to argue," Frank said. "That thing is moving!"

The dragon was heading toward them, swinging its massive tail from side to side as it came. Joe put his right foot into his brother's hand.

"Ready," Frank said. "One, two, three!"

Frank grunted and thrust him up the wall. At the same time Joe sprang off the ground with his left foot, straining for the top edge of the wall with his fingers.

He missed! His hands scraped the side of the wall but got nothing to grab. He came crashing down hard, and something gave in his right ankle. He reached down to grab it, his face twisted in pain.

"Are you all right?" Frank asked.

Joe struggled to his feet, shaking his head.

"My ankle. I twisted it." He leaned against the wall for support.

"We've got to try again," Frank urged.

Joe took a tentative step away from the wall and almost collapsed in agony. He wasn't going to be doing any more jumping that night.

"Can you support my weight?" Frank asked.

"I'll have to, won't I?" Joe said, glancing back over his shoulder. The dragon was about fifteen feet away, silently watching.

Joe cupped his hands. Frank jumped, caught the edge of the wall, and pulled himself up. When he lay across the top of the wall and reached for Joe's hand, their hands were a good half foot apart.

"You're going to have to jump!" Frank said. "I can't reach down any farther, or I won't be able to brace myself."

Joe turned around quickly to check on the dragon. It was moving again.

"I'm jumping," he said, gritting his teeth in anticipation of the pain. "I'm jumping."

He jumped and caught Frank's outstretched hand with both of his.

"Don't tell me how close that thing is," he said, planting both feet against the wall. Despite the pain in his ankle he made it to the top.

"You okay?" Frank asked.

"Pretty much," Joe said, catching his breath. He was exhausted. He looked down at the dragon, which was just beneath them. He shook his head. "Fido, the Komodo dragon. World's best watchdog."

"Come on," Frank said, lowering himself down the other side of the wall. "We're going back."

"Aren't we going to check for another way in?"

Frank shook his head. "Your ankle could be broken. We'd better get back to our room and see how bad it is."

Joe hobbled to the back door of the mansion. Frank punched in the code on the keypad there, and they stepped inside, finding themselves in the kitchen.

"At least we know there's something in that building worth protecting," Joe said. "Even if we can't be one hundred percent sure it's the bomb."

"It's not the bomb," Frank replied. "Not yet. But we do have to tell Endang about this place as soon as possible."

Joe nodded. "Hey, look," he said, pointing to a jar on the counter. He reached inside and pulled out a few more of the cookies Susanto had served them earlier.

"Just so the trip isn't a total loss," he said, crunching down on one while he held out another to his brother.

Frank shook his head and walked by Joe's outstretched arm. "You're hopeless," he said.

* * *

"I'm starving," Joe announced the next morning to Susanto. She was holding a platter of bacon, eggs, and English muffins.

The sun was streaming in through the kitchen window although it was only seven in the morning. Joe's ankle, it turned out, was only sprained, not broken. He told the others he'd hurt it coming out of the shower that morning—the nice, hot fifteen-minute shower he'd taken. Despite the pain he felt better and certainly cleaner than he had since arriving in Djakarta. On board the *Hatta* they took only lukewarm sponge baths to clean themselves.

Susanto handed him the platter, and he helped himself to his second huge portion.

"Anybody else?" Joe offered, holding out the platter. Krinski, seated at the head of the table, shook his head, as did Frank and Bob. Boris was too busy eating to look up, and Bill was sitting quietly drinking coffee. He wouldn't start eating peanuts till a little later.

Joe handed the platter back to Susanto. The whole situation felt weird. Here they were, a happy little family of Assassins gathered around the breakfast table, getting ready to blow up the world—or whatever—with their hydrogen bomb.

"You enjoy the breakfast?"

Joe smiled at Krinski. "It's delicious."

Krinski shrugged. "That's why I like Americans. You know how to enjoy life, how to live."

"It's easy to enjoy life when you have all the money in the world," Bob said.

"Well, we're all going to have plenty of money," Krinski said.

"How soon?" Joe asked.

Boris pointed his fork at Susanto. "Should she be here now?"

Krinsky shrugged. "She barely speaks English, but—as you wish." He clapped his hands and said something in Indonesian to Susanto. She bowed once, set the platter in the center of the table, and backed out of the room.

"How soon are we going to have plenty of money?" Joe repeated.

"I thought you were more concerned with avenging your girlfriend's death," Boris reminded him.

"I'd like to do both," Joe said, taking another strip of bacon from the platter.

"Well, don't worry," Krinski said. "You won't have to wait much longer. Of course"— he turned and stared at Boris—"if you'd brought Professor Stavrogin here instead of eliminating him, I could have finished up a whole lot faster."

Joe hid his expression behind another mouthful of food. He wanted to smile. He and Frank were the only ones at the table who knew that Stavrogin wasn't really dead. They'd saved the professor back in Alaska by pretending to kill him. He was with the Network now, safe and sound.

Bill frowned up from his teacup. "Stavrogin wouldn't have helped."

"We could have forced him," Krinski said. "Without someone to double-check my equations this could take another two days."

"If you're using a computer to check the equations, I can help," Frank said quietly.

"Really?" Krinski asked. "Which programs have you worked with?"

Frank rattled off half a dozen or so. Krinski looked impressed. "You can start this morning," the professor said.

"Hold on," Bob said, shaking his head. "We're all supposed to go back to the boat together."

"You can tell Nwali I insisted the boy stay," Krinski said. "If he wants to meet that ridiculous schedule of his, then I need help."

Joe had to stuff more eggs in his mouth to keep from smiling. This was the biggest break they'd had in the case yet.

"All right," Bob said reluctantly. He pushed his chair back from the table. "We'll contact you later in the day."

Joe followed the other three out the front door to one of the main avenues, where they caught a cab. By the time they reached the *Hatta* it was midmorning. Nwali was waiting for them.

"He is allowing the American to help with the

equations?'' Nwali shook his head. The leader clearly wasn't pleased.

"We tried to bring him," Bill said.

"Enough," Nwali said, and he turned to Joe. "I have a surprise waiting for you in your cabin, Joseph."

"For me?" Joe asked, puzzled.

Nwali nodded. "Come, I will show you. All of you, except Bob, please follow. Bob, go to the radio room."

He took Joe's arm and guided him below deck. The others followed a few steps behind.

Nwali said nothing, his eyes focused straight ahead. The younger Hardy was beginning to get a bad feeling about this.

"Here we are," Nwali said, opening the door to the Hardys' cabin.

Joe tried to keep his expression neutral. Sitting on Frank's bunk, holding an ice pack to her forehead, was Endang, appearing very small and very frightened.

A million thoughts flashed through Joe's mind. Had Endang talked, told Nwali she was with the Network? No. She was too much of a professional. But what was she doing here?

"Aren't you going to say hello to your friend, Joseph?" Nwali asked.

"Hello," Joe said simply.

"I saw her watching our boat from the pier

and had her brought here. She must be very anxious to see you again, don't you think?"

He continued without waiting for an answer. "Tell me, Joseph," Nwali said, "how is it that she knew where our boat was? Did you tell her?"

Boris stepped up beside him. "I can make him talk," the Assassin growled. "Give me five minutes alone with him."

Nwali held up a hand. "It's not necessary. I'm sure Joseph has a good explanation. Don't you, Joseph?" His voice was calm and reasonable. But his eyes were cold and dangerous.

"How did this woman find our boat?" He leaned in closer. "And what else have you told her about us?"

Joe swallowed hard, desperately trying to think of an answer.

Chapter

8

JOE OPENED HIS MOUTH with no idea of what was to come out.

Just then Endang jumped up from the bunk and ran into his arms. She began babbling in Indonesian.

"I do envy your skill with the ladies, Joseph," Nwali said. "One girlfriend dies, and you find another."

Joe saw red but restrained himself from striking out at the terrorist leader. Nwali was talking about Gina, but Joe was thinking about Iola Morton, his first girlfriend. She had died in the very first encounter he'd had with the Assassins, a victim of a car bomb meant for him and Frank. He'd almost forgotten how much he hated the terrorists for that, how much he wanted to destroy them.

He knew what he had to do.

Joe twisted his face into a sneer and shoved Endang away from him. She landed on the cabin floor and immediately began sobbing.

As Joe observed her he worked hard to keep himself from smiling. She should have been an actress.

"This girl means nothing to me," he said.

"But you know how we operate. You tell no one anything that might compromise our security." Anger crept into Nwali's voice. "You told this woman where to find us."

"I don't understand what's happening!" Endang burst out, tears streaming down her face.

"I made a mistake," Joe said, hanging his head.

"You did," Nwali replied. He stared silently at Joe for what seemed an eternity. "A fatal one."

Endang started crying again just as Bob entered the cabin.

"Krinski is on the line. He needs to talk to you immediately."

"Of course," Nwali said. "I'll be there in a moment."

Bob nodded and left.

"What do you suggest we do about your mistake, Joseph?" Nwali asked. "What do you suggest we do with this woman?"

Boris stepped forward. "The boy is useless," he said. "Let me—"

Nwali shook his head. "I asked Joseph."

Joe took a deep breath. He knew what Nwali wanted him to say. He knew how the Assassins operated, and he couldn't blow his cover. That would mean not only Endang's life, but his and Frank's, too. He had no choice.

"She means nothing to me," he repeated.

"Good." Nwali smiled. He reached into his waistband and pulled out a small pistol. "Then you won't have any problem killing her."

He handed the gun to Joe. "Will you?"

Joe swallowed hard.

"Of course not," he said.

It had been a long time since Frank had spent concentrated time in front of a computer screen.

He'd been running numbers for Krinski for close to three hours, keying in different variables for equations whose meanings only the scientist understood. The funny thing was, Frank wasn't bored. Two weeks playing solitaire were much more boring.

"Three more simulations to run," Krinski announced. He pushed his chair back from his computer and came over to stand behind Frank.

"I'm very impressed," Krinski said. "You certainly seem to know what you're doing."

"Well, Professor," Frank said, turning in his chair and looking up at Krinski, "so do you."

Krinski laughed. "You Americans. You're never afraid to say what you think."

Frank laughed, too, even though he hadn't

told Krinski what he was really thinking: You don't trust me, Professor, do you? You've left out any information that would help me figure out what the numbers I'm working with are intended to simulate.

What little Frank could deduce had to do with the rate of descent of a heavy object in a sort of thick, viscous fluid. How long would it take such an object to fall if it started off at ten miles an hour, twenty miles an hour, etc. There were a number of other variables in the equations as well, but Frank had no idea what they represented.

"I'm very pleased with the assistance you've provided me," Krinski said. "Very pleased. I may even ask Nwali to assign you to me for the duration of this mission." He folded his arms and stared at Frank. "What would you think about that?"

Frank smiled. "That would be terrific." But not for the reasons you think, Professor, Frank mused. It'll give me a better chance to figure out what you're up to.

"Well, then," Krinski said, "it's settled." He clapped his hands. "Susanto!"

The woman entered the room from the kitchen and bowed once.

"I'd like some tea," Krinski said. He turned to Frank. "For you?"

Frank shook his head.

"Very well," Krinski said. He returned to his

terminal and shut it down. "I'll be right back," he said. "I have a few things to take care of in the other building."

Like piecing together a hydrogen bomb? Frank thought. "Can I help you?" he asked, trying not to sound too eager.

Krinski shook his head. "I think I can manage. You finish up those simulations."

Frank smiled as he watched the man go. Krinski would be more than a little surprised at how good the work he'd been doing had been. While crunching numbers for the professor he'd managed to access portions of the computer Krinski had no doubt intended to be off limits to him, including a file marked Indonesia Simulation.

Now that sounded very interesting. Frank opened the file. Suddenly the screen came to life, filling with what appeared to be a map of the world. But this map had only one continent.

"Pangaea." That was Krinski's voice, coming from the computer. He must have put together this file as a presentation for someone. Nwali, perhaps? "Legendary supercontinent of two hundred million years ago."

As Frank watched, the single supercontinent drifted apart, forming into more recognizable shapes: Africa, South America, North America, Europe, Asia.

"Pangaea broke apart because of the movement of underlying geological structures known as continental plates." Now areas of each continent and its surrounding ocean were shaded in different colors.

"Even today continental plates are continually moving." Now the picture zoomed in on Asia. A dotted line appeared, circling a group of islands. The islands were Indonesia, Frank realized.

"This is the Java Trench, a place where two continental plates have collided. Their banging together resulted in the formation of the trench and left the area tremendously unstable.

"If a powerful explosive were detonated here, the result could be worldwide geological change."

A powerful explosive, Frank thought, his throat suddenly dry. Like a hydrogen bomb.

"This is the simulated result of one such explosion."

The screen went white. The light was so bright Frank had to shield his eyes. Then all at once the map of the world came back on screen.

Everything was different!

California was gone. The east coast of the United States had changed, and so had England and the Indian subcontinent.

Frank quit the simulation and sank back in his chair. So this was what the Assassins were planning. They were going to change the world—forever.

Chapter

9

JOE FELT SWEAT form on his forehead and trickle down his face. How was he going to get out of shooting Endang?

Nwali had left the cabin, Bill trailing behind him. Endang was still lying on the cabin floor, sobbing quietly. Boris was leaning against the door, arms folded across his chest. Joe knew that if he wanted to try to escape with Endang, he'd have to go right through the big man. He couldn't do it.

"Why are you waiting?" Boris demanded. "Shoot her!"

Endang raised her head to look at him with pleading eyes.

Joe's mind raced. With Boris standing over him he didn't have time to plan.

Joe jumped as the door to the cabin swung open. "We're returning to Krinski's mansion. Immediately!" Nwali announced. He walked up to Joe and took his gun away.

Nwali nodded to Boris. "Bring the girl. Quickly."

Joe tried hard not to show how relieved he was at not having to kill Endang.

At least not yet.

Frank struggled through the rest of the simulations Krinski had asked him to run, his head still spinning from the implications of what he'd found. He became aware of how much time had passed only when his stomach started growling and he noticed that another three hours had passed.

He was punching in the last numbers as Krinski entered the room.

"Tired?" Krinski was carrying what looked like a videocassette in his hand.

"A little," Frank said. "I finished running the simulations."

"Good," Krinski said, turning on his terminal. "Go ahead and shut down."

"All right." Frank pushed his chair back and stood up. "I think I'll get something to eat."

"Susanto has lunch ready," Krinski said. "We're just waiting for the others. They should be here momentarily." He smiled. "Why don't you have another cookie?"

Frank shook his head. "No, thanks. I'll hold off."

Frank knew that something was wrong. Krinski continued smiling at him.

"There are plenty left," the professor said. "Even after Joe's little raid on them last night."

Frank tried to act confused. "Little raid?" He forced a smile. "I'm not sure what you're talking about."

"Let's not play games," Krinski said. He reached inside his jacket, drew out a gun, and pointed it at Frank.

"I have cameras on all the doors. It's a security precaution," he said, holding up the videocassette in his left hand. "It's too bad I didn't have them on the other building, too. I'd love to see what happened when you met the dragon."

Frank pursed his lips. There didn't seem to be anything to say.

"Why don't you have a seat?" Krinski suggested, pointing to the couch in the center of the room. "The others will be here soon. Oh, I forgot," Krinski said, snapping his fingers. "You were hungry, weren't you? Susanto!"

The girl appeared at the entrance of the kitchen.

"Get our friend here a cookie," he said, still smiling. "In fact, make it a whole plateful."

Terrific, Frank thought, sitting on the couch. My last meal is going to be cookies.

Just then Nwali walked in. "You haven't

THE HARDY BOYS CASEFILES

changed the code on the front door yet," he said to Krinski.

"It hardly matters now," Krinski responded. "They won't be using it again."

As Frank watched, Endang stepped inside. Joe was a step behind her, strain showing on his face. The three other Assassins followed with guns drawn and leveled.

"What's she doing here?" Frank asked, pointing to Endang.

Joe saw the gun Krinski had trained on his brother and spun around to face Nwali.

"What's going on?" he asked. Suddenly Joe noticed that the Assassins' guns were pointed at him as well.

"You and your brother have betrayed us, Joseph," Nwali said.

"What are you talking about?" Joe said, shaking his head. "I've done nothing wrong."

Nwali nodded slightly.

Joe heard movement behind him, but before he could turn around something was smashed across the back of his head. He fell to the floor.

"Joe!" Frank called out.

"I'm okay," he said, struggling to his feet. Boris stood over him, his machine gun still raised like a club, a big smile on his face.

Krinski slipped the videocassette he held into a VCR. "I have an interesting little piece of video here. Let's all watch it."

Endang took Joe's arm and helped him over

to the couch, where they sat down next to Frank. The television screen filled with the image of the two Hardys walking downstairs and stopping in front of the keypad.

"Very clever," Krinski said, watching as Frank punched in the code. "How did you figure out the combination?"

Joe and Frank remained silent.

"It doesn't matter," Krinski said. "Here, this is my favorite part." He fast-forwarded the tape to the part where the boys returned to the house and Joe stopped in the kitchen. He froze the frame just as Joe was reaching into the cookie jar.

"I believe there is an American expression for this," Krinski said, and he started laughing. "You got caught with your hand in the cookie jar!"

"Enough." Nwali held up his hand. "We have decided you are spying on us. The question is why, and for whom."

"We're independents," Frank said. "For hire to the highest bidder."

Krinski smirked. "You seem a little young for that line of work."

"That's strange talk, Professor, coming from someone who graduated from college at fourteen," Frank said.

"We're older than you think," Joe added. "And the fact that we look so young makes us extremely valuable.'

Nwali sat down on the couch next to Frank and leaned back. "Who are you working for?" he asked, staring straight ahead. "The Network?"

"Meet our price and we'll tell you," Frank said.

"I think you misunderstand the situation here. You have nothing to bargain with. You either tell us what we want or we kill you," Nwali said matter-of-factly.

Frank shrugged. "You'll kill us, anyway. We're too dangerous—we know you're building a hydrogen bomb."

Nwali's eyes widened. For a second he was clearly stunned. Quickly he regained his composure.

"My compliments. Your appearances *are* deceiving." He stood. "And speaking of deceit . . ." Nwali walked around the couch to Endang and lifted her chin in his hand. "Who exactly are you, my dear?"

"She's just what she looks like," Joe said. "An innocent. Why not let her go?"

"I think not." The leader shook his head. "Now you all know too much." He turned to Boris. "Shoot them and throw their bodies in the canal."

Bob frowned. "If we don't want the bodies to float back to the surface, we'll have to weight them down."

"I have it!" Krinski said, motioning to Bob. "Get some of the large buckets we feed the dragon out of. They should be just outside the wall. Also bring some of the mixing cement from the garage.'' Bob nodded and left.

Krinski turned to Nwali. ''It's a good thing I watch so many gangster movies.''

Boris had left and now returned with some rope. He tied the boys' and Endang's hands behind their backs and led them outside, gun pointed, where Bob was waiting beside the cargo van in the ovenlike heat.

''Your last chance,'' Nwali said. He folded his arms across his chest and stared at each of them in turn. ''Tell me who you're working for, and I'll spare your lives.''

Endang, who had been silently whimpering since they'd left the *Hatta,* spoke up for the first time.

''I'm not working for anyone!'' she cried out. ''Why are you doing this to me?''

Nwali shifted his gaze to Joe. ''Joseph? Tell me who you're working for, and I'll let her go.''

Yeah, right, Joe thought to himself. He looked over Nwali's shoulder and saw Krinski standing there with a big grin on his face. ''Never'' was all he said.

''Kill them,'' Nwali said to Boris. He spun around on his heel and marched back toward the air-conditioned house to join Krinski and Bill.

The big Assassin slid open the side door of the van. ''Inside,'' he said, motioning with his gun. Joe sat down on the floor between Endang and a large bag of cement. Frank sat opposite them.

"I could find only two buckets," Bob said, pulling the van out of the drive.

"That's all right," Boris said. "The girl is small. If we tie a rock to her, she'll sink."

Endang started whimpering quietly. She was playing the part of the innocent perfectly, Joe thought, but he and Frank still had to distract the Assassins somehow.

They drove for maybe ten minutes before Bob pulled the van to an abrupt halt. Boris got out and slid the side door open. Now Joe was staring at a canal. It was only about fifty feet wide, with a small brick ledge running next to the water on either side.

"An excellent burial ground, don't you think?" Boris asked. "Come. Over here."

While Bob kept them covered Boris mixed up a small amount of cement in the two buckets. Then he put the buckets on top of the ledge and motioned to Frank and Joe.

"Step right up," he said.

Joe complied, Frank a step behind him. What else could they do? He and Frank were in way over their heads. Their only hope was that Endang had gotten some information to the Network. Maybe the Gray Man could pick up the Assassins' trail before they could use the hydrogen bomb they were building.

"Now step in the buckets, one foot at a

time," Boris said. He held the shovel he'd used to mix the cement across his chest and smiled. "You first," he said to Joe.

Joe did as he was told. It was like stepping into a giant vat of mud. But this mud was going to get rock hard very soon. He glanced over at his brother, who was also standing in a bucket of cement. Would Frank be able to think of a plan to get them out of this one?

"There," Boris said after about ten minutes. He stepped up on the ledge next to them, checked Joe's bonds, and smiled. "Now I think it is time for you to go swimming."

Frank leaned to his left, falling into Boris. Boris simply pushed him away, letting Frank fall facedown on the ground. He hit hard. With his hands tied and his legs encased in concrete he had no way to break his fall.

Nice move, Frank, Joe thought, because he knew Frank had just given Endang the opening she needed. The instant Frank moved, Bob's attention was taken from her.

Endang fell onto her back and slid her arms under her legs. A quick kick with her feet and her arms were in front of her. Even though her hands were still tied, she could at least use them now.

Bob turned at the noise just as she was charging him. She managed to knock the Uzi from his hands.

"You little—"

77

Joe watched as Endang spun into a vicious sidekick. Her foot caught the Assassin on the side of the head, and Bob crumpled to the ground, out cold. A quick somersault and Endang was standing with the Uzi in her hands.

The whole maneuver couldn't have taken more than five seconds.

"Untie them," she said to Boris. "Now."

Joe was impressed. "Wow," he said. "You really are a black belt."

Endang's gaze didn't move from Boris. "Did you think I was making it up?"

"I wasn't sure," Joe admitted. "But I definitely won't kiss you again without permission."

Boris still hadn't moved.

"You heard me," she said, raising the gun. "Drop that shovel and untie them."

"Of course," Boris said. He stepped back and then tossed the shovel aside. Right into Joe's stomach.

The sudden impact knocked him a little off balance, but that was all it took.

"Joe!" Frank cried out.

Joe heard Frank's call as he felt himself slowly tipping over backward. There wasn't a thing he could do to stop it.

Then he fell, and the cold water of the canal washed over him.

Chapter
10

FOR A SECOND no one spoke. Then Endang stepped forward and pointed the Uzi at Boris. "I ought to kill you right now," she said.

The Assassin laughed. "You don't have the nerve."

"And we don't have time," Frank said. Eight seconds had gone by. He'd started counting the instant Joe had fallen in the water. Joe could probably hold his breath for a minute—maybe a little longer if he'd had time to fill his lungs.

"Make him untie me," Frank said. "Then I'll take the gun. You bring Joe up."

Endang nodded, waving the Uzi at Boris. "Untie him."

Boris shrugged. "I don't think so."

"Do it!" Endang screamed. She fired the gun. The bullets carved up the ground around him.

Boris looked at her, shocked.

"Quickly," Frank said. In his head he was still counting. About twenty seconds had passed.

Boris untied him. Endang motioned him away and handed Frank the gun. Thirty seconds.

"Now untie her," Frank said. Boris did. Forty-five seconds. As she stepped up next to him on the canal wall Frank gave Endang the rope the Assassins had used to tie his hands.

"You'll never be able to pull him up, not with his feet trapped in concrete. Tie this around his body. We'll have to pull him out together."

Endang nodded and dived into the canal.

One minute.

One minute five seconds.

"Your brother is dead," Boris taunted. "And you're next."

"Shut up," Frank said. His back was to the canal. Just then he heard Endang surface behind him.

"It's too dark down there!" she yelled. "I can't find him!"

"Try again," Frank said, never taking his eyes off Boris. "He can't have moved too far from the wall."

He heard Endang dive back under.

Boris smiled. "Your brother is dead," he repeated, taking a step forward.

"I'm not even going to give you a warning

shot," Frank interrupted, his voice even and controlled. "Take another step in any direction and it'll be your last. If Joe doesn't come up alive," he said, lowering his voice, "you die, anyway."

Boris shrank back. Frank hoped the big man wouldn't call his bluff, although at this point he wasn't so sure it was a bluff.

Then he realized he'd lost count.

He felt helpless. Less than a dozen feet away his brother was drowning.

Endang surfaced again. "I found him!" She boosted herself onto the canal wall beside Frank, rope in hand.

"Use one of those branches," Frank said, nodding in the direction of a huge tree that overhung the canal. Endang draped the rope around the nearest and thickest branch she could find and began pulling.

"Wait a minute," Frank said. "I've got a better idea. Boris will pull."

The Assassin glared as Endang handed him the end of the rope. She held on to the line, too, feeding it to Boris as he began pulling Joe up.

Ten seconds later Frank heard his brother come up out of the water, coughing and gasping for air. Even though he wanted to turn and make sure Joe was okay he kept his gaze fixed on Boris the entire time.

"I've got you," he heard Endang say. Out of

the corner of his eye he saw her grab hold of Joe and lift him onto the edge of the canal.

"Let go of the rope," Frank told Boris. "And step back."

In one motion Boris tossed the end of the rope at Frank's face and dived to his left, into the forest.

Endang was after him like a shot. She returned a minute later, empty-handed and out of breath.

"He got away," she said, bending over to catch her breath, her hands on her knees. "I think that little dive into the canal took more out of me than I thought."

"Good riddance," Joe said as Endang untied his hands and broke the cement to get his feet free. "The guy was nothing but dead weight anyway."

Frank and Endang groaned simultaneously.

"Quick," Frank said. "Help me get out of this bucket before he makes any more bad jokes."

Four hours later Joe didn't even feel like smiling, much less making more jokes.

He poured himself another cup of tea and sank back into the plush hotel room couch. Endang sat next to him while Frank paced back and forth across the living room of the suite Colonel Mangkupradja had arranged for them. Joe couldn't understand why his brother was walking around. His feet must've felt the same as Joe's, he figured. They'd had to smash the concrete-filled buckets with the shovel to break free, and that had hurt.

It didn't hurt as much as blowing the case did, though.

After they'd gotten free Endang had walked up the main road, found a phone, and called for help. The police, led by Colonel Mangkupradja, had arrived shortly thereafter and taken Bob into custody.

Meanwhile, another contingent of officers had raided Krinski's mansion, only to discover that no one was home. The house was deserted, as was the building out back. The computers had been wiped. Even the dragon was gone.

And the *Hatta* had left port.

Mangkupradja relayed the bad news to them as they headed downtown in his staff car. Then he dropped them off at the hotel to shower and change, promising to return shortly. That had been almost an hour before.

Boris must have gotten back to Krinski's pretty quickly to enable the Assassins to move so fast, Joe thought. Nwali's terrorists must have been ready to move instantly, which meant that the bomb was close to being finished.

Now they'd lost their only lead to the terrorists.

All at once Joe stood and started pacing next to his brother.

Just then there was a knock at the door, and

two men walked in. One was Colonel Mangku-pradja. The other was the Gray Man.

He was the same as always, unassuming, unnoticeable. Maybe there were a few extra worry lines around his eyes, Frank thought, but considering what was happening, that wasn't surprising.

"Hello, boys," Gray said, taking a seat on the couch. "Ali"—he indicated Colonel Mangku-pradja—"has filled me in on what's happened. Good work."

"Good work?" Frank asked incredulously. "We've lost the Assassins."

The Gray Man shook his head. "You've flushed them from hiding, probably disrupted their schedule. It's only a matter of time now till we find them."

Frank hoped so.

"I have some other news you might be interested in," the Gray Man said. "Forrester's disappeared. Jumped bail."

Frank's eyes widened. That was a name he hadn't expected to hear again. Hank Forrester had been chief of security for Eddings Air in Atlanta, Georgia. The Hardys had discovered that he'd been involved with the baggage theft ring. For reasons that they'd never been able to establish, he had sabotaged the plane Frank and Joe had been flying into Atlanta, almost killing them in the process. Whether or not Forrester was connected to the Assassins was a question they hadn't been able to answer.

Someone else knocked at the door.

"Come in," the Gray Man called.

A white-haired man, lean and tanned, stepped into the room and shut the door behind him.

"News on the *Hatta*," he said. "She registered her next destination with the harbormaster here in Djakarta as the island of Krakatau."

Mangkupradja spoke up. "That's a very small port. I can set up a blockade that will catch anything larger than a rowboat trying to sneak in."

"Do it," the Gray Man snapped. He spoke to the white-haired man. "Get Deevers and Channing to coordinate with the colonel. I want them in Krakatau monitoring the situation."

The man was out the door almost before the Gray Man finished speaking. Mangkupradja, nodding goodbye, was a step behind him.

"Krakatau," Frank said thoughtfully. "That's very interesting."

"Why?" the Gray Man asked.

"You may know it better as Krakatoa," Frank said.

"The volcano!" Joe exclaimed.

"Exactly." Frank nodded. "It erupted about a hundred years ago, in the biggest explosion of the century."

"Krinski," the Gray Man said. "This is what I was afraid of."

"Hold on a minute," Endang said. "You've lost me."

"Remember that simulation I was telling you

about, on Krinski's computer?" Frank said. "Where an explosion triggered a massive seismological disturbance?"

"You're suggesting that they've found a way to trigger a volcanic eruption?" she asked.

Frank nodded, thinking back to the earthquakes in Alaska and the equations Krinski had had him run on dropping a small, heavy object through a viscous fluid. The Assassins were planning to drop a nuclear bomb into lava.

"Maybe not a volcanic eruption, but some kind of seismic disturbance."

"And Krakatau would be the perfect place to do it," the Gray Man said.

"Possibly," Frank said. "I don't know, though. It feels too easy."

"It's a place to start, if nothing else," the Gray Man said, peering at the Hardys closely. "You two look like you could use some sleep."

"Now that you mention it," Frank said, yawning, "it has been a long day."

"Why don't you hit the sack? Endang, your room is down the hall." He walked to the door. "Good night, boys. I'll talk to you in the morning. Good night," he said to Endang.

He shut the door after himself.

"I'm hungry," Joe said, clapping his hands together. "Anybody for room service?"

Endang yawned. "Count me out. I think I *am* going to get some sleep. Besides, they stop serving at midnight." She set her teacup down on the coffee table in front of the couch and stood. "Good night."

"Good night," Joe called after her.

After she shut the door he turned to Frank. "We could raid the hotel kitchen," he said.

Frank didn't even respond—he just glared. "Come on, let's get some sleep," he finally said.

"All right," Joe said reluctantly, "but this means a big breakfast tomorrow."

After they woke, though, Joe wasn't too hungry.

Along with a stack of new clothes piled high on the coffee table, he found a note.

Frank and Joe,

I appreciate your efforts on your country's behalf.

It was signed by Arthur Gray. Sitting underneath it were two plane tickets.

"He's sending us back to the States!" Joe exclaimed. "Who does that guy think he is? This is *our* case!"

Frank didn't say anything, though he was just as upset. Both boys liked to finish what they started.

"Come on," Frank said. "We're getting out of here."

"You said it," Joe replied, putting on the new

clothes that had been left for him. He stalked to the door, Frank a step behind, and threw it open.

Two men were standing there waiting for them. One was the white-haired man who had told the Gray Man about Krakatau the night before.

"Good morning," he said. "I'm Agent Drake."

The other man looked barely out of high school and had close-cropped reddish hair. "And I'm Rivers. We'll be escorting you to your flight." Both men smiled at the Hardys, and Frank forced himself to smile back.

"We'll be ready right after we get some breakfast," he said, and shut the door.

"Well, it looks as if the Gray Man is taking no chances. He's making sure we don't stick around," Frank said.

"We might as well eat, then," Joe said.

After breakfast Rivers and Drake led them downstairs to a waiting limousine, which took them to the airport. The two agents sat directly opposite the brothers in the waiting area by their gate.

Frank was sitting next to an elderly couple. "The kids' presents," he heard the woman say. "We have to get them out of that storage locker." She frowned slightly. "Do you still have the key?"

"I've got it. Don't worry," the man said. He

reached into his pocket. "I'll go get them. If I can figure out how this crazy things works."

He held out his hand. In it was a thick white plastic card.

Frank couldn't believe it—the card was an exact duplicate of the one he had taken from Butch before he died.

Chapter

11

THE ELDERLY MAN got out of his seat and began
walking down the concourse.

"Hey," Frank said to Rivers. "I need a candy
bar."

Joe stared at him strangely. "How can you
still be hungry after all that breakfast?"

"I'm a growing boy," Frank replied. "Can I
please go get a candy bar?" he asked again.

Agent Rivers frowned. "Drake will go with
you."

"Come on," Frank protested. "You've got
my brother here. You really think I'm going to
run away by myself?"

"You might," Rivers said.

Frank reached into his back pocket. "Here's
my wallet and my passport. Now I won't be able

to go anywhere.'' He slapped the two items into Rivers's lap. "Now can I please go without one of you guys hanging all over me?''

"Whoa,'' Rivers said. He smiled and held up his hands in mock protest. "I didn't know it was that important to you. Go ahead and get two candy bars if you want.'' Then his smile disappeared. "Just don't miss the plane.''

"I won't,'' Frank said. He got up out of his seat and hurried down the concourse, past a duty-free shop and a bookstore, looking for the elderly man. There was no sign of him.

Frank was about to give up when he turned the corner. There was the man, heading toward a roped-off section of lockers. A security guard was sitting at a desk next to them. Hanging over the lockers was a sign that said, in both English and Indonesian:

LONG-TERM STORAGE
EXPERIMENTAL CARD-KEY LOCKERS
PLEASE SHOW IDENTIFICATION

As Frank watched, the man handed the guard the white plastic card he was holding. The guard pushed it into an electronic reader on the desk, said something to the old man, and waved him past.

Frank stepped up and handed the guard his card.

"A-forty-three," the man said without looking up.

There were maybe several hundred lockers in the area. Each had a magnetic bar-code reader instead of the usual lock. Frank found number A43 and slid the card into the reader.

The locker popped open. Inside was a small metal case. With his back to the guard Frank pulled it out and flipped the lid.

A piece of brightly colored cloth lay inside, covering the contents. Frank pulled the cloth away, revealing a huge stack of cash—Indonesian rupees and American dollars—and a passport.

He opened the passport. It had Butch's picture, but carried the name Anton Lee. Probably another alias. There was also a piece of paper folded in the passport, with three English words written on it. "Bali" and "Hotel Sanur."

Frank smiled for the first time all day. They weren't off this case yet.

When he got back to the waiting area the plane was boarding and Rivers was furious.

"Where have you been?" he demanded, charging up to Frank as soon as he caught sight of him. "Don't tell me it takes fifteen minutes to buy a candy bar!"

"Relax," Frank said. "I'm here now." He reached into the knapsack he'd bought in the gift shop, pulled out a big chocolate bar, and handed it to Rivers. "That's for you. And here's one for you, too," he said, handing another bar to Drake.

Rivers handed Frank back his passport and wallet. "And those are for you. Have a safe trip home."

Frank joined his brother in line.

"Where'd you get the money for that knapsack?" Joe asked.

"I'll tell you in a minute," Frank said, a smile frozen to his face.

He gave his ticket to the gate agent and turned to see Rivers and Drake still watching them. He raised his hand and waved goodbye.

"We have to get off the plane without them seeing us," he said to Joe as they walked down the sealed gangway to the aircraft. Then he told his brother about the white plastic card and what he'd found in Butch's locker.

"Bali," Joe said. "That's where Nwali's from."

"Exactly." Frank nodded.

"Welcome aboard," the flight attendant said, checking Frank's ticket. "You're in the right-hand aisle, almost all the way back. And you're next to him," she said to Joe.

The two hustled down the aisle, right past their seats, and to the rear of the airplane. While Joe made a show of waiting to use one of the lavatories back there, Frank studied the food-service elevator.

Frank knew that the ground crew used the elevators to lift the food up to the main cabin. They were ridiculously easy to use, and they were big enough to hold two people.

"What's the plan?" Joe asked. "Do we ask them to let us off over Bali?"

"You have so little faith in me," Frank said, shaking his head. "What do you think I have in this knapsack?"

He let Joe take a peek.

"You're a devious fellow, Frank Hardy."

"Never mind the compliments," Frank said. "Ready?"

Joe nodded. "Ready."

"Snake!" Frank cried out, and he threw down the rubber toy he'd bought in the gift shop.

A dark-haired woman holding a baby in her arms took one look, screamed, and fainted. The flight attendant unloading the food-service elevator turned to help her. Within a few seconds the cabin was pandemonium.

Frank pulled out the cart in the food-service elevator, bent down, and stepped inside. Joe squeezed in next to him and shut the door. It was a very tight fit.

Frank reached around his brother and pressed the start button. They began to move downward.

"Now I know why plane food always looks so flat," Joe whispered.

The elevator stopped, and Frank pushed the door open and climbed out. He and Joe were standing on the runway directly beneath the plane. It was very loud and very windy.

A man in orange coveralls holding two yellow batons was looking at them strangely.

"Wrong plane," Frank said, backing away.

The man just stood there, mouth open.

"Yeah," Joe echoed. "Nice meeting you, though."

The man suddenly burst into a torrent of Indonesian and started waving frantically to another group of similarly dressed people about a hundred yards away.

The Hardys ran.

Frank and Joe bought a change of clothes at a shop in the airport and then boarded the next flight to Bali. Frank had purchased two tickets with the money in Butch's locker and was now reading a book about the island. Joe spent the brief flight sleeping.

Once they landed, a quick visit to the airport's information desk revealed that the Hotel Sanur was in the town of the same name on Bali's east coast. The easiest way to get there, according to the man at the desk, was to rent a car.

The drive took an hour, and the hotel was easy to find. It turned out to be a modest six-story building of concrete and glass. Joe gave the car to a bellhop to park, and he and Frank walked into the lobby.

"Can I help you, sir?"

"A room for two," Frank said. He gave the clerk the name on Butch's passport, Anton Lee.

The man behind the desk punched up some numbers on the computer before him. "Very good, Mr. Lee. I also have a message for you from Mr. Forrester. He's in room four-ten. Shall I ring him?"

"Oh, no," Frank said, trying to hide his excitement. What luck! They had found Forrester! "We'll surprise him."

"Very well," the clerk said, and he handed Frank a key. "You two will be in room five twenty-four."

Frank led the way there and opened the door.

"Wow," Joe said, stepping past his brother and entering the room. "This sure beats the cabin on the *Hatta*."

Frank agreed. Everywhere they turned there was another extravagance. The refrigerator was full of food and champagne. The bathroom had a Jacuzzi, the bedroom had two queen-size beds and a color TV, and there was another color TV in the living room, with a VCR and a selection of several of the latest movies.

There was a knock at the door. Joe opened it, and a bellboy walked in.

"I just wanted to make sure you were comfortable here," he said. His accent sounded Australian. "And to tell you about some of the activities taking place in the hotel this evening."

Before either of them could respond, the bellboy launched into his speech.

"There's a coed volleyball tournament starting at six, a Balinese *wayang orang* performance at eight, and disco dancing in the Livingston Lounge. Tomorrow morning at seven a tour bus leaves for Denpasar. And all week we have special transportation to the *Eka Dasa Rudra* ceremonies at Temple Besakih." He smiled. "Is there anything else you'd like to know?"

Frank pressed a wad of rupee notes into the young man's hand. "Thanks for your time," he said, opening the door. "Maybe we'll see you later."

"Do we check in with the Network?" Joe asked when they were alone.

Frank shook his head. "No. I'd like to find out more about what's going on here before we do that."

"Talk to Forrester, you mean."

"Right," Frank said. He picked up the phone and dialed Forrester's room. There was no answer.

"Guess we'll try later," he said, hanging up.

Joe smiled. "After that volleyball tournament."

"Wrong," Frank said. "The last thing we need is to get spotted by the Assassins. Then this trail will go cold, too." He opened the VCR cabinet. "Watch one of these if you want. I'm going to get some shut-eye." He yawned. It was barely past dinnertime, but he was exhausted. Frank put in a seven-thirty wake-up call.

The next thing he knew, the sun was streaming in through the window. Joe had fallen asleep on the couch with the TV on. They ordered breakfast and tried Forrester's room again.

"Nobody home yet," Frank said, hanging up the phone.

Joe took a big bite of French toast and stood up. "No sense in waiting around anymore. Let's check out his room, at least."

Frank nodded. A little careful snooping couldn't hurt.

They took the stairs down one flight, to room 410. There was a big Do Not Disturb sign on the door.

Frank knocked lightly, not expecting an answer. He wasn't expecting the door to swing open at his touch, either.

The first thing he noticed when he stepped inside was what a lousy housekeeper Forrester was. Room service trays littered the living room, and papers were scattered everywhere.

"Looks like we're talking about the same Forrester, at least," Joe said. He held up a baseball cap with the words *Eddings Air* stenciled across the brim.

Frank stepped into the bedroom. The TV was on, and a man was lying on the floor next to the bed.

"It's Forrester." Joe walked past Frank, bent down next to the man, and checked for a pulse. He shook his head.

"Make that, *was* Forrester."

Chapter

12

"WHAT NOW?" Joe asked.

"We don't have much choice, do we?" Frank knelt down beside his brother to examine Forrester's body. It was cold. The man must have been dead since the night before. There were bruises around his neck, as if he'd been strangled. "We have got to contact the police—and the Network."

"The Gray Man's just going to put us on another plane back to the States," Joe said. "And we're never going to get a chance to clean this mess up."

There was a knock at the door. "Housekeeping," a woman's voice called out.

Frank shook his head violently.

Joe nodded and cleaned his throat. "Come

back later," he said, in a voice as deep as he could made it.

He was rewarded with a burst of Indonesian from the woman outside, followed again by the announcement "Housekeeping."

"Go away!" he shouted, hoping that the maid would get the message from the tone of his voice, even if she couldn't understand the actual words.

"Housekeeping!" the woman repeated even louder, banging on the door again.

Great, Joe thought. He strode over to the door and swung it open. "Listen, come back in a while, would you?" he began even before the door was halfway open. "Fifteen minutes—"

He looked down, and his jaw dropped open.

Endang was standing in the doorway, wearing a maid's uniform and an expression of shock that probably mirrored his own.

"I might have known," she said. Before Joe could close the door she pushed the maid's cart inside and walked past him. "What are you two doing here?"

"We could ask you the same thing," Joe said, shutting the door.

"One of our agents spotted Forrester leaving the airport at Denpasar yesterday morning. We were hoping that he would lead us to the others. Unfortunately, he hasn't left the room since then."

"There's a good reason for that," Frank said. He nodded in the direction of the bedroom.

Endang brushed past him and returned a moment later.

"You didn't move the body, did you?"

"What do you think we are?" Joe asked indignantly. "Amateurs?"

"Have you learned anything from the Assassins? Any sign of them at Krakatau?" Frank asked.

She shook her head. "The Gray Man's been interrogating Bob for hours, but he hasn't said a word. As for the others, it's almost as if they disappeared off the face of the earth."

"So what's our next step?" Joe asked.

"Your next step?" Endang said incredulously. "Your next step is either a jail cell or a ticket back to the U.S. For real this time."

"Now wait a minute—" Joe began.

"Here's something interesting," Frank interrupted. He picked up a sheaf of papers from the floor next to Forrester's body and spread them out on the bed. Joe and Endang peered over his shoulder as he examined them.

"These are architect's blueprints," Endang said. "What would Forrester be doing with them?"

"Maybe he was planning to start a new career," Joe said.

"Maybe you—" Endang broke off speaking

and pointed to the TV. On the screen was a picture of a smoking volcano.

"What's that?" she asked, her voice strained.

Frank walked over and turned the volume up so she could hear.

"Experts are calling last night's tragic eruption of Gunang Api scientifically inexplicable," she translated almost simultaneously to the boys.

The camera pulled back. Everywhere people were crying, picking their way through the ruins of a small village.

"The devastation is complete. The historic island of Bandanaira, one of the fabled Spice Islands, has been almost completely destroyed by the eruption."

A sudden chill ran down Frank's spine. It couldn't be.

Endang sat down on the couch heavily and reached for the phone. She punched in a series of numbers, then hung up.

Ten seconds later the phone rang. She picked it up and whispered into it. Frank did hear her mention Forrester's name, though. Then she handed the phone to him.

"You've seen the news, I gather." It was the Gray Man.

"Yes, sir," Frank said. He motioned to Joe to pick up the extension in the bedroom. "We're both on the line now."

"I suppose I should be angry at you for slipping away from Rivers and Drake, but I can't really summon up much emotion for that kind of thing right now." He sighed heavily. "The Assassins' demands have just been delivered by courier. They claim responsibility for this eruption, saying that it was an example of what they can do without a hydrogen bomb. They want the U.N. General Assembly to come up with ten billion dollars by nine o'clock tomorrow morning, our time, or they promise that the next explosion will do a lot more damage."

"Can the U.N. raise that much money?" Joe asked.

"I don't know," the Gray Man said simply.

Frank remembered the simulation he'd seen on Krinski's computer, the new world that had been pictured after the destruction of the old. They couldn't be serious, could they? Would the Assassins really destroy the world if their demands weren't met?

"Frank? Are you there?" the Gray Man called.

"I'm here."

"Now, listen," the Gray Man said. "You boys were the last ones to have seen Krinski and Nwali. I want you to work with Endang. Try to remember what they said. Try to remember anything that could help us figure out where they are. Anything at all to help us stop them."

There was a sharp click and then a dial tone.

"Wow," Joe said, hanging up the phone. "I

guess he's not worried about us getting hurt anymore.''

"Why should he be worried about you now?" Endang asked, her voice soft and distant. "If we don't stop the Assassins, we're all going to die, anyway."

"That's a happy thought," Joe said.

"Well, I'm sorry." Endang got up and crossed to the window. "Cheer me up. Tell me something that will help us locate Nwali and his gang."

Joe shook his head. "I wish I could."

Frank took a deep breath and let it out slowly. The Assassins had been so careful about not letting him and Joe in on their plans that he couldn't think of a thing that might give them a clue to their whereabouts.

"Maybe Forrester left something important here," Joe suggested.

"That whoever killed him didn't take." Frank shook his head. It didn't seem likely.

He picked up the blueprints again and studied them. They were preliminary drawings with no writing on them anywhere, other than construction specifications. He couldn't figure out what they were for, either. It looked like a series of small huts arranged vertically, one on top of the other, along a large wall. The sheds were connected by a series of ventilation shafts and an elevator. That made no sense.

Frank flipped the papers over in disgust. In the upper left-hand corner, on the back, there was some writing. It was so small he had to squint before he could read what it said.

SMCS. Those were the same letters that had been stenciled on all those crates they'd moved.

"I found something!" Joe came out of the bedroom carrying a paperback book in one hand and a business card in the other. "He must have been using this as a bookmark."

He handed the card to Frank. It was for a company called Soeder-Masto Construction Supplies.

He smiled at Joe. "SMCS," he said.

For a second Joe didn't get it. Then his face lit up. "The crates we unloaded from the freighter and at Krinski's house!"

"Exactly," Frank said. "Let's contact the hotel staff and tell them about Forrester. Then we'll pay Soeder-Masto Construction Supplies a visit."

Frank found out that the company was located in Denpasar. According to Endang, it was about a fifteen-minute drive. Five minutes later she'd changed back into street clothes, and they were on their way. It was an hour before they reached the SMCS offices, which were located in a white two-story concrete building in the center of town.

"I can't believe all that traffic," Joe said, climbing out of the car.

"It's usually bad but not like this," Endang said. "Denpasar was a small town that became large almost overnight because of the tourist boom. The roads haven't caught up to the traffic yet. It's a lot worse right now because of the *Eka Dasa Rudra* ritual.''

''The bellboy at the hotel was talking about that, too,'' Frank recalled. ''It must be pretty important.''

''It usually takes place only once a century,'' Endang said. ''Religious groups from all over the island go to Temple Besakih for it. The ceremony's supposed to restore harmony in the universe and exorcise evil from this world. These are the last few days, too, so it's even more crowded. And considering what happened the last time they held it—''

''Let's do the history lesson later,'' Joe interrupted. ''Here's SMCS.''

''Let me handle this,'' Endang said, stepping forward. She gave a quick rap on the door.

Frank hung back in case there was trouble.

''Silakan masuk!'' a man's voice called out.

Endang pushed the door open.

A short, stocky man sat at a desk, his head down as he concentrated on his work. Papers littered his desk and covered almost every flat surface in the room as well.

Frank exchanged a glance with Joe. This guy certainly didn't seem like the Assassin type.

''Selamat pagi,'' Endang said.

The man finished writing and raised his head. ''Ah, Americans.'' He came around the desk and shook their hands. ''Very pleased to meet you. My name is Batal Kouri. Kouri to my friends. I am president and chief operating officer of Soeder-Masto Construction Supplies. Also vice-president and chief financial officer." He smiled. "What can I help you with?"

"I'm Endang Merdeka." Then she introduced Frank and Joe. "I'm with the Indonesian government, Mr. Kouri. These young men are with the U.S. State Department, and we're investigating some illegal smuggling of construction supplies out of this country."

Kouri seemed confused. "What does that have to do with me?"

Frank stepped up. "We've traced some of the material back to your company. We'd like to see a list of the people you've sold various supplies to over the last six months or so."

Kouri frowned. "We deal with only the most reputable clients, I assure you."

"We're not trying to imply that you've done anything wrong, Mr. Kouri," Endang said quickly. "We're just looking for a place to start."

Kouri nodded. "I understand." He turned around and started flipping through the papers on his desk. "Ah. Here we are." He pulled out a thick stack of pages that had been stapled together and started riffling through them. "Hmm. Hmm."

He turned back to the three of them. "There are only five projects we are currently supplying where I do not know the builder personally. Two are hotels on Irian Jaya. A high-rise in Djakarta. A guest house here on Bali, near Besakih. And an addition to the sultan's *kraton* in Yogyakarta."

Frank shook his head. That didn't help them much.

"Do you have a list of what was ordered?" Endang asked.

"Of course," Kouri said. He put the papers back on his desk and turned to the filing cabinets next to them. He flipped through the drawers, pulled out several manila folders, and handed them to Endang.

Frank and Joe peered over her shoulder as she scanned the contents of each folder in turn.

"Most of those pages," Kouri said, "contain site specifications. The list of actual supplies ordered is on the yellow paper stapled to the back of each folder."

Frank nodded. There were also photographs of the proposed sites in each file, he saw as they went through them. The high-rise in Djakarta was going to be built in the middle of a whole block of similar buildings. One of the hotels in Irian Jaya was going to go up in the middle of some of the most spectacular, pristine wilderness Frank had ever seen.

Endang opened the folder for the guest house in Besakih. Frank saw that it wasn't scheduled for completion until later that year. Too bad. With all the activity around there because of that big religious ceremony, they probably needed another guest house now.

Endang flipped another page, and there were a photo of the site.

It looked like a beautiful setting. There was a series of pagodas in the foreground set against lush forests and a towering mountain peak.

Frank suddenly realized he'd seen that view before. For a second he couldn't remember where, though. Then all at once it hit him. That night aboard the *Hatta*, when he'd surprised Nwali and Bob in the ship's computer room. This was almost the exact image.

He reached over Endang's shoulder, pulled the photo out of the folder, and took a closer look.

"It's a volcano," he said quietly.

His brother and Endang turned around to face him.

"What?" Joe asked.

Endang looked at the picture Frank was holding. "You're right. That's Mount Agung, the highest peak on Bali. Those structures are at Temple Besakih."

She paled as she realized what Frank was suggesting.

"Agung erupted during the last *Eka Dasa Rudra* ceremony. It's been dormant for almost thirty years."

Frank looked at her. "But not for much longer now."

Chapter
13

"THIS IS UNBELIEVABLE," Joe said. "You're sure we're heading to the right place?"

His brother nodded. Joe really didn't doubt Frank. He knew Frank was right the second he'd identified Agung. A big enough explosion there would trigger worldwide seismic disturbances just like the ones Frank had seen on the professor's computer simulation. An explosion at this place would cause exactly the kind of "change" Nwali had been talking about back in Djakarta. Though he still didn't know why the Assassin leader was so keen on change, Joe liked Indonesia the way it was—not split in half by a hydrogen bomb.

Normally, he wasn't in favor of rewarding terrorists, but Joe really hoped the U.N. could come up with the ten billion dollars.

Kouri had told them the guest house was being "built" by a man named Anton Lee, the name that had been on Butch's passport. Lee was supposedly on site now, in a small village called Selat. After thanking the man, they'd gotten back into their car and started the journey there. The only problem was that Selat was on the way to Besakih. From the jammed roads ahead it seemed as if everyone else was on the way to Besakih as well.

At least Joe was getting a glimpse of an entirely different world. The scenery was spectacular. The road climbed upward toward Mount Agung, passing through lush rain forests and several small villages. At one point there was enough of a break in the forest to see all the way down the mountainside to the ocean, several miles away.

Along the road people were on the way to Besakih. Whole villages were traveling together, Endang said. Joe saw women in colorful sarongs, and men in shorts and shirts and turbans, holding umbrellas and carrying offerings for the *Eka Dasa Rudra* ceremony.

"Check that out," Joe said. Ahead of them a number of women were walking along with jugs the size of medicine balls balanced on their heads. "Those things must weigh close to twenty pounds each."

"Probably more," Frank said. "And they're getting to move faster than we are."

"Selat. Here we are," Endang said as they passed a large sign. She pointed at a food stand just ahead. "Pull in there. I'll see if they know anything about a construction site."

The stand consisted of a grill and several benches. Endang went up to the man behind the grill and spoke with him.

"We have to take that side road over there," she told Frank and Joe when she returned to the car. "He says there's something going on down a dirt road off the main road, about an hour away. He wasn't sure this car would make it."

"We could do it on those," Frank said, pointing to a pair of motorbikes parked by the food stand. Two young men, about fifteen or sixteen, were leaning against them, wolfing down food.

"It's worth a try," Endang said. "I'll talk to them."

Joe watched as she started talking to one of the boys. He smiled and nodded as Endang pulled something out of her handbag and showed it to him. Then she pointed up the road toward Agung.

He listened to Endang, then shook his head. Endang said something else. He shook his head again. She threw up her hands in exasperation and walked away.

"What happened?" Joe asked.

"I told him I was a government agent and that I needed to requisition his vehicle."

"And?"

"And I don't want to tell you what he said."

"Let me try," Frank said.

"His name is Haji," Endang called after Frank. "For all the good that will do you."

Frank walked over to the boy and pointed to the motorbikes. Haji shook his head. Then Frank reached into his pocket and pulled out a handful of bills, which he held out for Haji to take. Haji's eyes widened a little, and he waved his friend over.

"We'll bring these back in a few hours," Frank said. "Do you understand?"

The young men exchanged glances and nodded.

"You got a deal," Haji said in clear, almost unaccented English. He took the money.

"Watch our car, too," Joe said.

"You got it, boss," Haji said, smiling. He walked away with his friend.

"Mission accomplished," Frank said, climbing on one of the bikes. "Let's get going." Endang slid on behind him, and they were off.

The road was unpaved and clearly used infrequently. Rocks and other debris from the forest often blocked their path. They kept having to ride around outcroppings of blackened rock that sometimes stretched for several hundred feet, like hardened streams.

"What are those?" Joe called ahead. He was riding behind Frank and Endang.

"Lava flows," she called back. "From Agung's last eruption."

Joe noticed the forest thinning out as they continued. He realized that they'd probably gone up a thousand feet in elevation. Every few hundred yards or so there would be a break in the forest canopy, and he could see Mount Agung looming above. It was probably just his imagination, he thought, but at one point he thought he saw the top of the volcano actually smoking.

Suddenly he heard a loud noise like a gunshot.

"What was that?" he asked.

Up ahead Frank had pulled off the road.

"Flat tire," he said disgustedly, climbing off the bike. He examined the front tire and shook his head. "And there's no spare. I'm going to have to go back to Selat to get this fixed."

"I could take the tire, get it fixed, and ride back," Joe said.

Frank shook his head. "Then three of us are sitting around waiting. It's already getting late." He looked up at the sun, which was starting to set. "We don't have a lot of time to find this place before dark. You two had better go on ahead."

"All right," Joe said reluctantly. Endang climbed on behind him. "If we don't find anything, we'll meet you back at that roadside stand."

"I'll catch up to you!" Frank called after them as they pulled away.

Ten minutes later Joe and Endang found the construction site.

They almost missed it. In fact, Joe had already ridden by when Endang tapped him on the shoulder.

"On the right!" she said, pointing behind her. "I think I saw something."

Joe made a U-turn and went back. Sure enough, barely visible was a small dirt road. The entrance had been blocked by a chain strung between two trees. A sign hung from the chain.

" 'No trespassing. Construction site,' " Endang read. "Bingo."

They got off the bike and wheeled it around the chain, then hopped back on and continued down the road for about a quarter mile. The road ended in a clearing. Joe knew they were nearing the Assassins' hideout, and he certainly didn't want the motorbike announcing their arrival so he hid it in the trees. They continued through the forest on foot till they came to the edge of the clearing.

Joe stopped and looked at the area before him. It was an airstrip. Directly opposite it was a small shack made of corrugated steel with an overhanging steel roof and a single pull-down door. A small wooden dolly sat in front of the door.

Pacing back and forth in front of the shack was a man in tan shorts and shirt with what looked like an assault rifle strapped to his chest. As Joe watched he pulled a handful of peanuts out of his pocket, cracked the shells open, and began eating them.

"It's Bill," Joe said.

"This is it," Endang said. "Your brother was right."

Joe nodded, then cocked an ear upward. "Did you hear something?"

Endang frowned. "No."

"Look." Joe pointed across the horizon. "It's a helicopter, and it's coming down here." He and Endang crept farther back into the woods.

As they watched from behind the cover of trees the helicopter landed. Two men Joe had never seen before got out and shook hands with Bill. Then one of the men went back into the helicopter. Joe saw Bill wheel a dolly underneath the copter's cargo bay, and a crate was lowered onto it.

"This must be their drop-off point," Endang said. "They're probably ferrying supplies from here up the mountain."

Even from this distance Joe recognized the SMCS logo stamped on the crate. He also saw something in Indonesian stenciled across it in red.

"I've seen that crate before," Joe whispered to Endang. "Frank and I opened it in the *Hatta*'s cargo hold." Joe took a deep breath. "Inside is part of the nuclear reaction chamber!"

"Let's go," Endang said.

"What?"

"We have to tell the Network about this."

Joe shook his head. "We can't just leave," he said. "Think a minute. They're supposed to set off the bomb tomorrow morning if they don't get their money."

"So?"

"So we have to stop them before the bomb is finished and in place. And that crate contains a piece they absolutely need to finish it."

"You've got a point." She nodded grudgingly. "What do you suggest?"

Joe watched as the three men wheeled the crate into the shack. The two newcomers emerged a few seconds later, climbed into their helicopter, and flew off.

"We circle around and wait behind the shack. They'll need to fly in another helicopter to move it up the mountain. When they do, we move in on them."

"It's too dangerous," Endang said, shaking her head.

"And letting them get away with the piece they need to finish building the bomb wouldn't be?"

Endang stared at him a minute. "All right," she said finally. "Let's go."

They made their way through the forest to an area just behind the shack and waited.

About twenty minutes later Joe heard another helicopter approaching. Under the cover of its landing they crossed the short distance between the forest and the back of the shack. After the copter's engines cut off he heard the sound of familiar voices. Boris. Nwali. Bill. And another, fainter voice he couldn't quite place.

The door to the shack opened and closed again. He nodded to Endang.

"Let's do it," he said.

They burst out from behind the shack on opposite sides of the Assassins. Boris and Bill were standing in front of the shack, talking.

"Freeze!" Endang called out, drawing her gun.

Joe rushed forward and grabbed Bill's assault rifle out of his hands.

Surprise registered momentarily on Boris's face, instantly replaced by a look of cold hatred. "You!"

Joe smiled. "You peeked." He knocked on the door of the shack. "Whoever's in there, come on out with your hands up."

The door to the shack opened. A split-second later Nwali appeared, followed by a girl.

It took Joe's brain a few seconds to register what his eyes were telling him. The girl was Gina Abend.

She was alive.

118

Chapter

14

"GINA! HOW—" Joe shook his head in confusion.

"Don't move," Endang said, waving her gun in the Assassins' direction. "Joe, who is this?"

He couldn't answer. He was still in shock. Gina was alive. It couldn't be! The Assassins had said she'd died in a hail of gunfire back in Alaska, trying to save his life. They had lied—of course they had lied.

Gina ran to him. Before Joe's mind could register what was happening, she was embracing him.

"Joe," she said.

He was really confused.

As Endang took a step forward Boris dropped to the ground and spun his legs to the left, sweep-kicking her feet out from under her. She fell to the ground, and her gun went off harmlessly.

"Endang!" Joe shouted.

Something hit him across the back of the neck, and he stumbled forward. Gina stepped out of his way, and he fell to the ground. Someone stepped on his wrist and took away the gun he was holding. He heard the crystal on his watch shatter.

Then he heard Gina laugh.

"Why did you do that?" Joe asked Gina, climbing to his feet. "I don't understand."

"You're such a fool," Gina said. "What don't you understand?"

He looked at her, and the truth hit him.

"Gina is one of us," Nwali said. "She has been from the beginning."

Joe's mind reeled. "Even when we were working with you in Atlanta and Alaska?"

"I tried to have you killed before you got to Atlanta," Gina said. Her voice was cold and far harsher than Joe remembered it.

"Eddings's plane," Joe said. "You sabotaged it!" He and Frank had almost died that day. Only Solomon Mapes's skill as a pilot had saved them.

"But how did you know about us?" Joe asked. Gina laughed.

"The Assassins always know what you and your brother are up to. Did you really think you had us fooled all this time? That we were such amateurs?" Nwali asked. "We were playing with you. It made us laugh to watch you react."

"I should have taken care of the plane myself rather than trust that fool Forrester," Gina added.

"You killed him," Endang said.

"*I* killed him," Boris said, a light dancing in his eyes.

"The fool got greedy," Nwali said. "As if we hadn't paid him enough to deliver the case with Stavrogin's notes to us." He turned to Endang. "Though I suspect I'm not telling you anything you don't already know. How is Gray, by the way?"

Endang shook her head. "Who?"

Nwali laughed. "And, Joseph, where is your brother?"

Joe shook his head. "I have no idea."

Nwali rammed him in the stomach with the butt end of the machine gun.

Joe gasped, the wind knocked out of him, and bent over double.

"No more unpleasant surprises, Joseph. Is he out there," Nwali pointed to the forest, "waiting for us?"

"I already told you," he said, struggling to catch his breath. "I have no idea where Frank is."

Nwali held the machine gun pointed at Endang's head. "Now do you have an idea?"

Joe shook his head again.

"Talk," Boris commanded, stepping in front

of Joe. He drew his right hand back and punched Joe in the jaw. Joe fell to the ground.

"He's useless now," Joe heard Gina say. "Let's get rid of both of them."

"Not yet. We may still need hostages before this is over," Joe heard Nwali say. "Let's finish loading the helicopter. Professor Krinski is anxious to complete his work."

Joe rolled over and looked up.

The sun was setting behind Mount Agung.

Night was already falling as Frank rode back up the mountain. He missed the dirt road on his way up, and it was pitch-black by the time he turned around and finally found it.

There was no sign of Joe or Endang.

The road ended in a clearing with a small shack in the center of it. It was completely deserted. Frank turned on the flashlight he had bought in Selat and pointed it toward the shack. His beam fell on something on the ground on front of it. He bent down and looked closer.

Peanut shells. Had Bill been here?

He must have been. That meant the Assassins had been here, too. So where were they now? And if this was the construction site, where were all the supplies Kouri had sold the Assassins?

He walked back out on the main road, shining his flashlight left and right. Finally he found some tracks on the left side of the road and traced them into the forest.

Something reflected off his flashlight. Chrome. Joe's bike. So Endang and Joe had found this place, too. Where were they now?

There were only two possible conclusions: His brother and Endang had been kidnapped, or they'd been killed.

He rode back down to Selat. The roadside stand had closed, but Haji was still there, waiting by their car.

"Where's the other bike?" the young man asked.

"Where's your friend?" Frank countered.

"He got tired and went home. Nothing happened to that bike, right?"

"It's fine," Frank said. "We'll go get it in a minute. But first I need to use a phone." He wanted to contact the Network.

"There's no phone service here," the young man said.

Frank nodded. It figured. He'd have to rescue Joe and Endang on his own. He thought a moment. Krinski's equations called for dropping a hydrogen bomb through lava. To drop something you had to be fairly high up, right?

He looked at Haji. "I need to get up the mountain. To the top."

"Up Agung?" Haji shook his head. "The crater's been closed for the last three months. The government decided it was too dangerous."

"Really?" Frank asked. He bet he knew whose money had helped them make that decision—the Assassins'. "Then I definitely have to go."

Haji shrugged. "I can take you, but we'll have to do it on foot. No roads go all the way up. And we'll have to wait until morning. The trails are too dangerous at night."

"I have to go now," Frank said. He needed the cover of night and the advantage of surprise when he came upon the Assassins.

The young man eyed Frank. "You're wearing shorts. Do you know how cold it gets up in the mountains?"

Frank shook his head.

The young man pointed toward Agung. "That's three thousand meters high. Ten thousand feet. Why do you have to go there now?"

Frank smiled. "I'll tell you on the way."

Haji rode with Frank up the mountain until they came to the other bike. Then the two of them took a back road to his house in Sebudi, a small village a little farther up the mountain.

His mother tried to talk them out of climbing the mountain at night, but when she saw that they weren't going to listen she made them some strong coffee and gave them a knapsack full of snacks. Frank also borrowed long pants and a sweater from Haji. By the time they set off it was close to midnight.

"You were going to tell me why you have to climb Agung tonight," Haji said. There was a full moon, so he was able to set a brisk pace for them. As he walked his breath turned to steam in the night air.

"Where'd you learn to speak English so well?" Frank asked, changing the subject.

Haji smiled. "Cable television. I worked at one of the tourist hotels down south for three years. Then I quit and came back here. Now I am taking a correspondence course with an American institution.

"Really?" Frank asked. "In what?"

"Computers," Haji said. "I want to marry an American girl and work for a big company." He pointed to the side of his head. "I have big ideas."

For the next hour or so they walked up the mountain along a dry streambed, talking about computers. Then they came to another village. Haji sat down on the ground, pulled out a canteen, and drank.

"Have some," he said, offering the canteen to Frank.

"No, thanks. I'm not thirsty."

"You'd better drink," Haji told him. "From here it gets tough."

Frank held out his hand and took the canteen. He took a swig and handed it back to Haji. "Let's get going."

Those were the last words he spoke for the next hour and a half. The trail went almost straight up. Frank found that he needed all his breath just to keep up with Haji. As they walked the forest changed from tropical vegetation to pine trees.

Then the trees disappeared, and they were staring up a steep, rocky climb to Agung's summit. The wind was blowing, and for the first time since he'd left Alaska Frank felt cold.

Haji pointed up. "That goes straight up to the crater wall. There's a breach at the top that leads you in."

"Thanks," Frank said. "I think I can manage from here."

"You want me to leave you?" Haji shook his head. "How are you going to find your way back down?"

"My brother's up there," Frank said. "I'll manage." He shook Haji's hand. "Thanks."

Haji shrugged. "Have it your way." He handed Frank the knapsack of food. "Good luck."

"Thanks," Frank said again.

He turned and started the long ascent to the top of the mountain. The way up was all shale and loose volcanic rock, and incredibly slow going. By the time he neared the top the sun was starting to show over the horizon.

He scrambled up the last few yards to a narrow path that circled the crater wall. He found the breach in the crater wall about two hundred yards to his left. There was a yellow sign on it, with writing in both English and Indonesian: Danger.

The thought occurred to him that the Assassins might have planted the sign to hide what was going on inside the crater. If that was true, he was about to walk into the middle of a very risky situation.

On the other hand, maybe the Assassins weren't involved at all. Maybe the crater was simply too unsafe to explore.

Either way, Frank knew he couldn't win.

He took a deep breath and stepped forward.

Chapter

15

THE VOLCANO was alive.

Frank could feel the heat coming off it. He looked down and saw that he was standing on a narrow trail, about three feet wide, that ran inside the crater. Steam rose from the massive pit beneath him. Frank sniffed the air, and the smell of sulfur bit into his nose.

The Assassins were here, and so were their supplies. Just as they'd done in Alaska, they had brought an inactive volcano to life, probably using a series of small explosions to rekindle it.

This time Frank knew that the Assassins weren't going to stop at small explosions, though. No, this time they were planning to cause a major volcanic eruption.

Frank knew that this was the Assassins' grand

plan. They had probably been working on this for months. He looked at the incredible structure laid out before him. Now he knew where all the construction supplies they'd bought from Kouri had gone.

The terrorists had built right up against the crater wall, using it as the foundation for a series of six small, interconnected structures stacked one on top of the other at roughly five-foot intervals. The largest was at the bottom and appeared to be about twenty feet square. At the rim of the crater was a helicopter pad.

Forrester's blueprints, Frank realized, were preliminary sketches for this place.

Ladders covered the crater wall between each building and ran to the helicopter pad at the top of the rim. A series of rails for the elevator, he remembered, ran from the helipad down, past each of the six structures. But the rails didn't end there. They continued down inside the volcano and disappeared into the crater below.

That's how they're going to lower the bomb, Frank thought. All right, then. He had found the Assassins. Now he had to find Joe and Endang.

A light snapped on in one of the sheds. Through a window Frank saw a figure. He rubbed his eyes. Could it be? Frank focused his eyes on the window again. Yes, it was true. He was looking at Gina Abend. She was alive!

The Assassins must have been lying about her death all along. Joe and Endang were probably being held with Gina in the same shed, then. At last, a lucky break.

Rescue one of them, and he'd rescue all three.

Joe couldn't sleep.

It had nothing to do with the concrete floor or the gusts of wind that whipped through the crack between the bottom of the door and the floor. He'd slept in worse places. The problem wasn't physical. It was mental.

He couldn't get over the expression on Gina's face when she'd called him a fool. He'd let himself be used by a girl who didn't care for him at all. Now it was going to cost not only his life, but the lives of a lot of others as well. Unless the U.N. could come up with the money. They'd have to, wouldn't they?

Gina had thought so last night after they'd landed on top of the crater complex. "They'll get it," she said. "Now that we've proven the kind of destruction we can cause."

Krinski had been waiting for them as the helicopter landed. He actually smiled as Boris led Joe and Endang, both with their hands tied securely behind their backs, off the plane.

"Good to see you again, Joe," Krinski said. "Sorry I can't offer you any cookies, but"—he shrugged—"them's the breaks, as they say."

Joe shook his head. "Give it a rest, will you?"

"This is the last crate, Professor," Nwali said.

"I believe you have everything you need now to complete the bomb."

"Have it brought down to the lab," Krinski said, focusing on Joe and Endang. "You're very lucky. You're about to see history made."

Joe watched as Nwali clenched his teeth at Krinski's offhand order to have the crate moved. There was definitely tension between those two, he observed. He hoped he'd get a chance to play on it at some point.

"The only thing these two will see for the moment is the inside of the supply shed," Nwali said. "I want them securely out of the way until morning. We'll know if we have any further use for them by then."

Boris grabbed hold of Joe with one hand and Endang with the other and dragged them forward and into an elevator car at the edge of the helipad. As they descended Joe peered through the gate into the crater below.

The elevator ran from the helicopter pad at the top of the rim down the inside of the crater wall along two steel rails. The crater complex was impressive. They passed three small buildings set into the crater wall before they stopped at the fourth.

Boris slid the gate open and shoved them forward into the supply shed. It was a bare room, its only light coming from a line of fluorescent bulbs in the ceiling. Most of the shelves were empty.

"Looks like you're not planning to stay too long," Endang said, glancing around.

"Neither should you," Boris replied. "Of course, if it were up to me, you would be in that volcano already."

"They don't let you decide anything, do they? Poor boy." Joe shook his head. "Just because you're not very smart."

The big man smiled. "I'm smart enough not to let some girl throw her arms around me while I'm trying to fire a gun."

"What girl would want to throw her arms around you, anyway?" Joe shot back.

Boris smiled and backed out of the shed. "We'll see you in the morning. Get a good night's sleep." The smile disappeared from his face. "It will be your last."

"Aren't you at least going to untie us," Endang asked, "so we can move around a little?"

Boris shook his head and slammed the door shut behind him.

"He's right," Joe said. "I blew it big time. How could I have let Gina trick me like that?"

"She lied, Joe," Endang said. "Your only crime was believing what she said."

"I was an idiot."

"It's over and done with," she insisted. "Come on," she added, sitting down against the wall, "let's get some rest."

Joe sighed and sat down next to her, but he couldn't fall asleep. His thoughts kept turning to

Gina—how she'd tricked him, how Bill had gotten his gun back, and how Gina had shattered the crystal in Joe's watch.

If only he could get at a piece of it and use it to cut through his rope.

He stood and walked to the opposite wall, then drew his hands back and slammed the back of his wrist directly into the wall. He was rewarded by the sound of a tiny piece of the crystal tinkling to the floor.

Across the room Endang woke up. "What was that?" she asked groggily.

"Nothing," Joe said. He sat down on the floor and reached for the broken crystal. "Go back to sleep."

She obliged.

He sat back down against the opposite wall and started to work on the rope.

Frank stopped to catch his breath. He'd had to go back through the breach in the crater wall and climb to the summit of Mount Agung to get to the helicopter pad.

The sun was just starting to rise as he stepped onto the asphalt surface. He took the last of the food Haji's mother had packed—a handful of rice and meat in a spicy peanut sauce, wrapped in a banana leaf—out of the knapsack and swallowed it in two bites. He was running on adrenaline now.

Frank leaned over the edge of the helicopter

pad and looked down. The shed Gina and the others were trapped in was about thirty feet down. He didn't have a rope, and the inside of the crater wall was too sheer to climb. All the ladders ran through each building. The last thing he needed to do was run into Boris right then.

That left the elevator. He couldn't use it even though the car was right in front of him, waiting. The noise would alert everyone. But the rails the elevators ran on—that was another story.

He examined them closely. They were about four feet apart, offering a gap big enough to wedge himself between and shimmy down to the building he wanted. Of course, one slip and he'd end up as lava soup. He didn't want to think about what would happen if someone summoned the elevator while he was climbing down.

Still, what choice did he have? Slinging the knapsack over his shoulders, Frank lowered himself from the edge of the helipad and dangled over the crater below.

He moved his feet around until they banged into one of the elevator support struts. He wrapped his legs around that and shimmied down the strut until he was flush against the crater wall. From there he swung into the gap between the two rails, pressing himself tightly between them.

Then he began climbing down. It took close to half an hour to reach the entrance to the third shed. Grabbing onto one of that building's support struts, he swung himself into the narrow door frame.

Slowly he forced the elevator door open.

Gina was standing there, shock written all over her face. "Frank! How did you get here?"

"It wasn't easy," he admitted. "Where's Joe? And Endang?" There was a door to another room at the end of the shed. He walked past Gina and entered it. It was a bathroom, with the access ladder he'd noticed before running through it.

"You've come to rescue me," Gina said. "Haven't you?"

Frank was a little confused. "This doesn't seem like a prison cell."

"It isn't," Gina responded.

Frank didn't have a good feeling about this situation. What was going on here? Why was Gina acting so strangely? Slowly he turned and found himself facing the barrel of a gun.

"But I'll be happy to show you to a cell in a minute," Gina said, a smile spreading across her face.

Chapter

16

"I'M SO GLAD you could join us," Nwali said to Frank. "With you here, our little family is all together again."

"What have you done with my brother?" Frank asked. "And Endang?"

"Don't worry," Nwali said. "They're resting comfortably. Why don't you relax and enjoy your surroundings for now?"

Frank looked around the room they were gathered in. Gina had told him it was Krinski's lab, the last and biggest of the structures inside the crater wall. After capturing Frank Gina had summoned the elevator and brought him down there immediately. Boris, Nwali, and Krinski were already in the lab, waiting.

Seeing the Assassins again didn't really shock

Frank. What shocked him was the bomb. He and his brother were about to witness the Assassins' grand finale. No, Frank thought, he had to find a way to stop them.

Frank studied the bomb the Assassins had created. To Frank it looked like a fancy piece of medical diagnostic equipment, something you might see a technician wheeling down any hospital corridor. It was about a foot high and six feet long, with an industrial gray casing. On the outside was a clock with a digital counter. Red numerals reading 00:00:00 kept flashing on and off.

"I see you've noticed our little surprise package," Krinski said. "You'll be happy to know it's completely ready to go. We've used conventional explosives to reach the magma layer, and now all that remains is to lower the bomb into the crater."

"It'll be too bad if the U.N. decides to pay your ransom and you don't get to try your bomb, though."

"The explosion at Bandanaira already proved my theories," Krinski said. "My share of the money would suit me just fine right now."

"Why haven't we heard from them yet?" Gina asked. The clock on the wall opposite her read eight-thirty. "They've only got another half hour."

As if one cue, a buzzer sounded softly. Nwali crossed the room to a video monitor embedded in the wall and pressed a button. Bill's image filled the monitor.

"A message is coming in from our agents in Zurich," he said. "The U.N. representatives have agreed to pay."

"Is the money in our account?" Nwali asked.

"No, but they assure us it will be there by the end of the day."

"Not good enough," Nwali said. "Tell them we need the money in half an hour, or we detonate."

Bill seemed to be surprised, and suddenly the monitor went blank.

"Come in," Nwali said. He twisted a knob on the console. "Come in!"

There was no response.

"Very convenient timing," Nwali said. He turned to Frank. "You brought others with you."

Frank shook his head. "No. I have no idea what's happening either."

The terrorist leader spoke to Krinski now. "Professor, prepare the bomb for immediate launching."

"But they've agreed to pay," Krinski said.

"Do as you're told," Nwali snapped. He backhanded the professor across the face, and Krinski stumbled and fell to the floor.

"You fool. They've said they'll give us the money. What more do you want?" Krinski got to his feet and straightened his clothing. "I insist we at least reestablish contact with them."

"*You* insist. I see." Nwali nodded to Boris. "Kill him."

Before Frank could move, or before Krinski could react, the Assassin drew his gun and fired. Krinski crumpled to the ground again. This time he wouldn't be getting up.

"No one, and nothing, is more important than our goals," Nwali said. His eyes scanned each of the Assassins in turn. "Is that clear?"

"Perfectly," Gina said. Then she smiled. "Besides, now our share of the money is bigger."

She still didn't get it. Frank had seen the horrifying truth in Nwali's eyes when he ordered Krinski's death. The Assassin leader wasn't interested in money—he wanted to set off the bomb.

He took a hesitant step forward. If he could get Nwali's gun—

Nwali whirled. "Not so fast. Step back." Frank obliged, and the leader turned to Gina again. "Get the elevator. We will have to lower the bomb ourselves."

"If they don't give us the money, you mean," she said. There was a slight crack in her voice as she walked to the doorway and pressed a button. Maybe she realized Nwali's true intentions now, too, Frank thought.

"And then check on our prisoners. Use the access ladders. You go with her," he commanded Boris. "It's time to tie up all the loose ends."

"You mean kill them?" Boris asked, a smile spreading across his face.

"Yes," Nwali said. "Yes, that's exactly what I mean."

After an hour of whittling away at his bonds with the piece of crystal from his watch, Joe had managed to free himself and Endang. They were still trapped inside the shed. Then he'd spotted the air ducts in the ceiling and remembered something from the blueprints Forrester had been carrying.

"These run between the buildings," he said. He was able to boost Endang up into the shaft. He watched as she wedged herself in the shaft and began shimmying up. Then she disappeared from sight.

The next thing he heard was a yell of surprise and a loud thump. Then nothing.

A cable shot down from the ventilation shaft.

"Come on up," Endang called down. "The coast is clear."

He pulled himself up into the next building and saw what she was talking about.

Bill was on the floor, out cold. Endang was sitting before a shortwave radio holding a transmitter and frantically twisting knobs.

"This is their communications center," she

said. "From here we ought to be able to reach the Network."

She tried for five minutes to get the system working. Nothing.

"Here," Joe said, taking the transmitter from her. "Let me try."

Just then a door at the rear of the structure swung open, and Boris and Gina stepped through, both carrying guns.

"Well, look who's here," Joe said. "Our couple of the month. Mr. and Mrs. Psycho."

"Get away from that transmitter," Gina commanded. "And get your hands up. Both of you."

"There's no need for that," Boris said. "We're just going to kill them, anyway."

He raised his gun and pointed it straight at Joe. "Right now."

"I don't think you ever wanted the money," Frank said to Nwali. "Why? What do you hope to accomplish by blowing up half the world?"

"You're mistaken, my friend. I would have taken the money," Nwali said, "if they'd given it to me on my terms." With one hand he held a gun on Frank, and with the other he wheeled the bomb into the elevator.

"But I don't look at the world the same way you do," Nwali continued. "I was born an Indonesian, born into a country held hostage by Dutch colonialists for three centuries. When we finally became independent I saw the almighty Western dollar take us hostage all over again."

He looked at Frank. "I would have taken the money. But what I want most of all is change."

"Destroy a country to change it?" Frank asked. "That makes no sense."

"Sometimes it is the only thing that does make sense," Nwali replied. "Tear something down to start all over again. And Indonesia will not be the only country destroyed by this explosion."

"I've seen Krinski's simulation," Frank said.

Nwali nodded. "Then you know the entire world will be different after today. America, Europe, Africa. No place on earth will escape untouched."

"You're crazy," Frank said. "Millions will die."

"And millions more will be born into a better world. A world without superstitions like the *Eka Dasa Rudra*. When people believe such foolishness they can never have real power. Like the *wayang kulit* and the *dalang*," he said. "In the world of *wayang* the *dalang* is king. But outside that world he is just a man."

He shook his head. "My father was a *dalang*, and the Dutch killed him as easily as you or I would stomp on a bug."

Frank was finally beginning to follow Nwali's twisted logic. He realized there was no way to talk the Assassin out of the decision he'd just made. In a sense, Nwali had been preparing for this moment all his life.

"Now, this," Nwali said, pointing at the bomb, "this is the ultimate truth, the ultimate power."

Nwali pressed a button on the clock, and the display on it changed to read 00:30:00.

"Thirty minutes till it explodes," Nwali said. "Come, Frank." He held the elevator gate open. "Let's take a little ride."

Chapter

17

"DROP THE TRANSMITTER," Gina ordered.

Joe put the transmitter down by slamming it into the console. Sparks flew from it, and lights all across the room dimmed.

"You idiot," Gina said.

"Enough," Boris said. He squeezed the trigger.

Endang moved, diving and rolling to the other side of the room, somersaulting again and again. Boris changed targets quickly, trying to follow her. Gina turned and took aim at Endang, too.

Joe had to stop them. He hurled himself through the air at Gina, batting away her gun and knocking her to the ground. He dived over her, reaching for her weapon. She leapt after him just as Boris fired.

The bullets caught her in midleap.

She screamed once and fell to the floor.

"Gina!" Joe cried out, turning.

Boris brought his weapon to bear on Joe again.

Endang came up behind the big Assassin and slammed him over the head with a chair. He fell to the ground, and Endang picked up his gun.

Joe knelt beside Gina and felt for a pulse. "Nothing," he said, stunned. "She's dead."

This time she really was dead. He felt hollow inside. Gina had tried to kill him, so why he should feel anything at all for her was beyond him, but still . . .

Endang laid a hand on his arm. "Joe, I'm sorry."

A sudden noise made them turn just in time to see Boris dash into the room from which Joe had entered.

"The access ladder!" Endang shouted. "He's going to get away!"

Joe rose to his feet. "Not if I can help it."

The elevator was open on three sides with a rail running around the cage at about waist height. As they descended, moving closer to the bubbling crater below, Frank started to feel nervous. On the climb up the mountain Haji had told him stories about Mount Agung, calling it the abode of the gods. Right now it seemed as though the gods were angry. Agung was churning even more intensely than he had remembered.

"From here it's very simple," Nwali said as they came to a stop. They hung about twenty feet over the crater. "We disconnect the elevator from all other controls by pressing this, then." He held his fingers poised over a button. "By pressing this we detonate explosive charges calculated to send the bomb into the lava at the correct velocity. And the rest, as the professor would have said if he were here"—Nwali smiled—"is history."

"If you do this thing, there will be no history," Frank pleaded. "Do you know how many people are going to die because of this explosion?"

Nwali shrugged. "People die all the time. You have to look at the larger scheme."

There was a sudden jolt as the elevator began moving upward.

"That's impossible," Nwali said. "They know not to interrupt the launch sequence."

Now it was Frank's turn to smile. "In the larger scheme of things," he said, "I think that means that you're alone."

"No," Nwali said, turning toward the control panel. He slammed a button, and the elevator came to a stop. "I won't be stopped now!"

Frank saw his chance. He kicked out, and the gun went sailing out of Nwali's hand and into the bubbling crater below. "Now we're evenly matched," he said.

Nwali turned and smiled at Frank. "Evenly matched?" The terrorist shook his head. "I think not. Twenty-five minutes," he said, reading off the time registered on the bomb's display. "I think you'll last for no more than five minutes."

Frank suddenly realized the man was right. He hadn't slept at all the night before. There was no way he was could last more than five minutes, not against a disciplined fighter like Nwali.

Without warning Nwali launched into a series of sidekicks that drove Frank against the cage wall.

Frank stepped forward and swung. He missed, and Nwali followed with a flurry of punches that sent him crashing to the floor. Blood trickled from the side of his mouth.

"Not even five minutes," Nwali said, looming over him. "Pathetic."

Frank looked up at him, gasping for breath. His gaze bore into the Assassin's. "Tell me, Assassin. What would your father think of you if he could see you now? What would he think of what you're trying to do here today?"

"Now you're a psychologist, is that it?" Nwali said, suddenly angry. "Get up. Let's finish this."

Frank struggled to his feet. He knew he looked done, but he wasn't. Not quite yet. He had one good swing left in him.

Frank pretended to sway, and Nwali grabbed him by the collar of his shirt. Frank smiled at the man.

"You have nothing to smile about," Nwali said, drawing back his fist.

"That's what you think," Frank said. He swung with everything he had. His right hand connected with Nwali's jaw, and the Assassins' eyes rolled up into his head. He crumpled to the ground, unconscious.

Frank took a deep breath and leaned on the railing, looking out over it into the crater below.

Maybe it was his imagination, but he thought the gods seemed a little less angry than before.

Boris had too much of a head start. He was going to get away, Joe realized.

Instead of continuing when he reached the helipad, the Assassin paused at the top of the ladder.

"I'm waiting for you, Hardy," he called down. "Come up without your gun, and I'll fight you." He smiled. "And then I'll throw you right into the crater."

"Tough talk," Joe said.

He scaled the ladder as fast as he could. He wanted to fight Boris, too. He knew it didn't make any sense, but he blamed him for Gina's death. It was easier, he guessed, than blaming himself.

"All right," Joe said once he was within

reach of the Assassin. "Step back onto the helipad—"

Boris slammed his foot down hard on Joe's right hand.

His fingers exploded in agony.

"Idiot," the Assassin said. He started climbing back down the ladder, raising his foot again to stomp on Joe's other hand. "Why should I fight you fairly?"

Joe held his right hand to his chest and tried to back down the ladder. But he knew he couldn't go fast enough to get away from Boris.

"Hold it right there," a voice said, "or I'll blow you away."

Boris stopped. Joe looked up to see Haji, the kid who had rented them the motorcycles, standing behind Boris. He was holding a rock up against the Assassin's head. Boris, of course, couldn't see that it was a rock.

Joe forced himself not to smile.

"Don't turn around. Just step back up toward me," Haji said. "That's it, nice and slow."

Joe followed them up and got another surprise.

Two more helicopters were sitting there. One was full of police, who quickly surrounded Boris.

"Look who's here," Endang said, climbing up behind Joe. She pointed to the other helicopter.

The Gray Man and Colonel Mangkupradja stepped out and jogged over to meet them.

"It's all over," the Gray Man said. He took turns shaking their hands. "Good work."

"Not quite," Joe said. "Frank's still down there."

Just then the elevator rose up from below. The gate swung open, and his brother emerged.

"Where's Nwali?" Joe asked.

Frank nodded toward the elevator. "In there, with the bomb." He turned to Mangkupradja and the Gray Man. "You've got about twenty minutes to disarm it."

Mangkupradja nodded. "I can handle that." He barked out a series of orders, and a squad of police immediately formed up around the elevator. Two men in white lab coats climbed out of the same helicopter the Gray Man and the colonel had emerged from, and they entered the elevator.

"They'll take care of it," Mangkupradja assured them all.

"How'd you find us?" Frank asked.

The Gray Man and Mangkupradja pointed to Haji, who smiled.

"The police like to know who's climbing the mountain," Haji said. "I told them some crazy Americans were running around up there."

"Ali and I put those reports together with your disappearance," the Gray Man said to Endang. He shrugged. "It doesn't take a genius to get four when you add two and two."

"It did take some quick decision making to

bring the police in," Mangkupradja said. He put an arm around Haji's shoulders. "Let's talk about what line of work you plan to go into."

"Sure," Haji said. The two of them began to walk toward the waiting helicopters. "Do you know anyone in the computer industry?"

"Nice work again, boys," the Gray Man said.

"When are you going to stop calling us boys?" Frank asked.

The Gray Man laughed. "Come with me and we can talk."

Frank followed him.

That left Joe and Endang alone.

"It was great working with you," he said.

"Same here." She smiled. "Look me up the next time you're in Indonesia."

"I will," Joe said. She stood on tiptoe and kissed him on the cheek. "Goodbye."

"Goodbye," Joe said. Then Endang turned and walked after Mangkupradja and Haji.

He watched as the police brought up Gina's body and loaded it into one of the copters. He still felt bad about what she'd done to him, but more than anything he felt sorry for her.

He walked after the Gray Man.

"I don't know where your brother went," the Gray Man said, leaning against one of the helicopters. "He was here just a second ago."

"Frank?" Joe looked around but didn't see him anywhere. Finally he spotted him at the top of the crater, looking down the mountain.

"You see that?" he asked Joe as his brother joined him, pointing down the mountain. Far off in the distance there was a splash of vibrant color.

"Yeah," Joe said. "What is it?"

"Temple Besakih," Frank said. "The last day of the *Eka Dasa Rudra*." He smiled. "The exorcism of evil."

"We did our part," Joe said.

"That we did." Frank clapped him on the shoulder. "Come on. Let's go home."

Two days later they were back in Bayport, and things were pretty much back to normal.

Callie Shaw, Frank's girlfriend, was babysitting a neighbor's son for a week while his parents went on a second honeymoon.

She had brought Eddie over to Frank and Joe's house for that afternoon because the kid really liked Joe.

Right then Eddie was pouring baking soda out onto the dining room table. He called it a science experiment.

"Hey, take it easy with that stuff," Joe said. "You'll ruin the table."

"It's an experiment, Joe," Eddie said. "It's really cool. Just watch."

The doorbell rang.

"Hold on a minute, Eddie," Joe said. He went to open the door. Vanessa Bender was standing there.

"Glad to see me?" she said.

"You bet," Joe replied. He turned to Frank and Callie. "What do you say we hit the mall? I'm dying for a pizza."

"Sounds good to me," Vanessa said.

"Wait, Joe." Eddie had some vinegar out now. "Watch this."

He poured the vinegar onto the baking soda. The entire mess erupted right there, all over Mrs. Hardy's table and floor.

"Boom!" Eddie cried out. "See? Just like a volcano!"

Joe's face went white.

"What do you think?" Eddie asked, beaming up at him.

Joe shook his head. "I think whoever came up with that experiment has a sick sense of humor."

Vanessa and Callie looked at him strangely.

"You're too sensitive, brother," Frank said.

"Maybe," Joe said. "But let's get out of here before Eddie starts on his next little experiment."

Frank laughed.

Frank and Joe's next case:

Joe's girlfriend, Vanessa Bender, has introduced the Hardys to an old family friend, Brett Cooper. Brett is the pilot and designer of *Brett's Beauty*, the high-powered piston-engine prop plane set to compete in the upcoming Bayport Unlimited Air Races. But while he's aiming to break the world speed record, someone else has targeted him for terror!

The key to the case is the mystery of Brett Cooper himself—his hidden past, his hidden enemies. For Frank and Joe, the investigation quickly turns into a crash course in danger as they fly blind into a web of blackmail, sabotage, and murder. They're about to learn that in a world of daredevil pilots and death-defying stunts, the risks can be sky-high . . . in *Danger Unlimited*, Case #79 in The Hardy Boys Casefiles™.

Most Archway Paperbacks are available at special quantity discounts for bulk purchases for sales promotions, premiums or fund raising. Special books or book excerpts can also be created to fit specific needs.

For details write the office of the Vice President of Special Markets, Pocket Books, 1230 Avenue of the Americas, New York, New York 10020.